Bedti

for Kids

Let Your Child Discover an Imaginative World Full of

Dinosaurs, Unicorns and Adventures

to Help Them Fall Asleep Fast Feeling Calm

Uncle Teddy

Copyright 2022—All Rights Reserved

This book belong to:

Follow us on Facebook

for lots of free daily content

Your Free Gift

As a thank you for your purchase, we're presenting you "Activity Book," a printable book with drawings of your favorite dinosaurs to color, a sudoku section to improve math while having fun, and a word search section for memory and visual recognition

The whole family can continue to have fun

together.

Click this link to free download

https://BookHip.com/CLCHDQA

Table of Contents

Introduction

It may not sound surprising that reading to kids has significant developmental benefits for them. But did you know that a child's third-grade reading ability is a crucial determinant of future academic success? If they cannot read proficiently by the end of third grade, they are four times substantially less likely to graduate high school. Fortunately, you are an excellent parent who is prepared to instill in them an early appreciation for reading, right?

When preschoolers were read aloud, the regions of their brains responsible for visual imagination and narrative interpretation were active, according to one study. This indicates that their young imaginations were active as they constructed their interpretation of the story being read to them. In contrast to watching television or movies, reading requires children to use their imaginations; consequently, they develop a greater appreciation for a well-written story.

After a full day of playing, running, and wasting energy, youngsters must relax. Putting them to bed and wanting them to go asleep immediately can be fairly challenging, but establishing a nightly routine where you read them a tale can help them relax, calm down, and reduce their stress levels, which will result in better sleep.

Because they must interpret a narrative when it is read aloud, children become more imaginative. Children gain the power of their imagination, which enables them to become independent readers of non-picture books in the future because their imaginations are developed enough to captivate them.

One of the nicest gifts you can give your kids is a love of reading. Reading bedtime stories has so many benefits that the list might go on for years. This book contains the best bedtime stories that will inspire your children to create their own worlds.

Chapter 1: Stories about Unicorns

1.1 The Missing Unicorn

L uke loves animals. His favorite subjects in school have always been animal-related. He adored every single one of them, from zebras to aardvarks and everything in between; he adored large, terrifying dinosaurs and small, adorable bunnies. Luke enjoyed tigers and lions, antelope and deer, hounds and foxes, spiders and snakes. Well, let's say he liked all creatures. But one day, Luke observed something that caused him some concern. One species was never mentioned whenever he read about animals in books, visited the zoo, or studied them in school. One creature he had never even seen in a photograph: a unicorn.

Luke was worried. Why was the unicorn not mentioned in any of these story books? Why did his instructor never discuss unicorns? Why, when he questioned the zookeeper for directions to the unicorns, she gave him a stern look and walked away while muttering something about "clever Aleck kids"? When he questioned his father why he was told that there were no unicorns in the area where they were fabricated. Luke, however, could not comprehend this. Why would someone invent an animal when the world is filled with so many incredible ones? It simply looked absurd. Moreover, if you had to invent an animal, why would you invent something as basic as "a horse with a horn"? Nope. It did not add up. Luke had never questioned his father, a question he could not answer in his entire six-year existence because Luke's father was one of those clever types. If his father did not know about unicorns, he reasoned that certainly, no one did. Therefore, he determined that it was his responsibility to answer this enigma.

Luke's grandmother and grandfather resided on a farm, and he would occasionally visit them. This time, he was especially looking forward to going because he had some searching. As soon as he arrived, he started questioning the animals about their knowledge of unicorns. Since they were animals, Luke was not surprised that none of them spoke to him. At this point, he began to believe that he had not considered this good plan. But, c'mon. He is just six! That evening, Luke's grandfather inquired,

"Why were you speaking with those pigs earlier?"

I wanted to learn if they had any knowledge of unicorns.

"Eh, unicorns?"

Luke informed his grandfather about his investigation. Pop-Pop was one of those cool old guys that enjoyed games and adventures, so he said,

"I've got a plan to crack this case wide open!"

Therefore, he brought Luke into his home, and they conducted an Internet search for "unicorns." According to material discovered by Pop-Pop on the Internet, unicorns were initially referenced in Greece before spreading to Europe and Asia. They are mentioned in Arthurian legends and the Bible. Although the creature's appearance varies according to culture, his basic form is consistent: At least one long, pointed horn on the forehead of a horse or horse-like animal. Even the British Royals incorporate a

13

unicorn into their family crest. All of this was amazing, but it didn't explain why Luke couldn't discover any unicorns! Luke had learned much about the mythology of unicorns by the time he went to bed, but nothing that would help him locate a genuine one. He was dissatisfied as Grammy tucked him into bed. As he shut his eyes and drifted off to sleep, he began to believe unicorns were fictitious.

"Hey, Luke? Luke? Are you awake?"

He opened his eyes and saw a unicorn standing next to his bed, with white fur that appeared to sparkle. It had a long, shining tail with a tuft at the tip, similar to a lion's, a goat-like beard on its chin, sparkling eyes, and, of course, a gleaming golden horn on its forehead.

"I've heard you've been searching for me", the unicorn remarked.

Luke whispered in wonder, "I thought you were playing a role!"

"Oh, no, not really. Truth be told, Luke, we unicorns like to be left alone. Therefore, when the Ancient Greeks found us and began alerting the rest of the world about us, we attempted to flee and find another secret location to reside. But wherever we went, people who had known of unicorns pursued us. We traversed India, Europe, and China in search of a location where we might be alone."

"But why do you desire solitude?"

"It's simply our custom, Luke. Everyone is unique and has distinct preferences. Some creatures, like humans, enjoy interacting with

14

numerous other species. Some, like us unicorns, choose a serene, secluded life of introspection among our kind. Do you understand?"

"I believe so."

"However, after all these millennia, we've finally discovered a location where we can live quietly and calmly, unbothered by humans or other animals."

"Where?"

"I'm afraid I can't tell you. It has been a secret for many years, and I cannot reveal it for fear of its exposure."

Luke begged the unicorn not to tell, and he even made the largest pledge in the world, swearing he would never reveal the secret to any woman, kid, man, or animal as far as he lived. The unicorn answered, "Very well," before leaning in and whispering into Luke's ear.

"Ohhh!" said Luke. In retrospect, it made complete sense.

"However, you must never attempt to locate us, Luke. You must honor our privacy requests and leave us all alone. You promise?"

"I will cross my heart. Mr. Unicorn, thanks for reaching out. Now that I understand you folks are okay, I feel better."

"Thank you, Luke. For having such concern for us. Now you better get asleep, and I better go home. Great night, dear friend".

Luke shut his eyes and resumed sleep. Luke honored his word and never revealed the existence of unicorns as far as he lived. Even though he knew precisely where to locate them, he never attempted to visit the location to see for himself. Luke was the first human in a century to witness a real unicorn, and that was plenty for him. And even as he aged into extreme old age, he never forgot his commitment to the unicorns. Therefore, they remain secure in their hidden hiding place in - ah! Sorry, it's a secret!

1.2 The Unicorn and His Friends

Once upon a time, a beautiful island existed. In the island's meadows resided a beautiful fairy named Isotopia. She kept a monkey named Lola as a pet. Isotopia and her monkey were simple creatures with plain tastes and a simple lifestyle. They resided in a modest home with little furnishings. On the same island lived a Unicorn with the extraordinary capacity to fly very far and high. The only desire of Isotopia was to ride a Unicorn someday. She was home alone one day when Lola went to eat bananas. As he climbed a banana tree and began to eat, he noticed that the Unicorn was standing below. He was observing him. Lola was not your average monkey. He was extremely intelligent and able to communicate with every creature on the island. He also threw bananas at the unicorn and asked, "Would you permit me to ride on your back one day?" The Unicorn responded, "You've fed me delicious fruits. You can undoubtedly rely on me". Lola was thrilled! He leaped upon the Unicorn's back, which took off into the sky. Enjoyed very lot by Lola. When the unicorn landed, Lola expressed gratitude for the

16

ride "I could never have imagined how unique this experience would be! I am Lola. Which is your name?" The Unicorn introduced himself as Euno "Will you be my companion?".

Lola responded, "Of course, I'll be your pal." They played cooperatively. Late at night, Lola bid goodbye to Euno. When he returned home, he informed Isotopia about the unicorn.

She uttered, "Oh! How wonderful! I wish I could also ride on him! Will you please take me to the Unicorn tomorrow, Lola?" Lola complied with her request. The following day, while they went and met Euno, they saw that five evil men had bound him with a rope and were forcing him to follow them. Isotopia inquired, "Why are you treating the poor Unicorn this way?" One of the men responded, "Speak no word, girl!" A unicorn is quite uncommon! We are Lucky to encounter him. We will make a fortune off of him". With these words, the man pushed Isotopia away. The five evil men then abducted Euno. Isotopia and Lola felt sorry for the Unicorn, but the five men from the island's neighboring town were notorious for their infamy, so Isotopia and Lola chose to remain silent. They knew the men's residences. They devised a strategy to save Euno. As night fell, they traveled to the men's residence. Then, they added a sleeping medicine to their lunch in secret. Only two men consumed the meal and fell into a deep sleep.

The three remaining men dined outside and slept in a separate room. Isotopia secured the exterior door of this room. Now, Lola attempted to loosen the rope that was securing Euno. However, the rope was tied quite tight. Therefore, when Lola attempted to cut the rope, Euno was injured and cried out in anguish. Three men awoke, but two continued to sleep deeply. They realized that Euno's pals had arrived to free him, but their door was barred from the exterior. They began pushing and banging on the door, and after a few minutes, they could break it down and escape. When they emerged, Euno's rope suddenly came loose. The men ran at them, but Isotopia and Lola scrambled onto Euno's back to escape. One of the men clutched Lola's tail, but when Euno began to fly, he released to go and fell to the ground. All the men regarded them with rage and dismay, but what could they do? During their voyage, Lola introduced Isotopia to Euno. The Unicorn also became close to Isotopia. Lola and Isotopia suddenly observed that Euno was falling to the ground and had transported them to an unfamiliar location. They shut their eyes due to the extreme brightness of the light. When they reopened their eyes, they realized they had approached a massive, golden-lit palace.

Lola and Isotopia were stunned by what they saw. Lola questioned Euno, "Where are you taking us?", "This castle belonged to my parents", remarked Euno. "Where are they?" questioned Lola. "They may no longer exist, for all I know." Euno spoke mournfully, "About six months ago, they had left for the jungle one day and never returned." However, perhaps they are yet alive! said Isotopia. "How I wish what you say were true", Euno murmured. A sound suddenly emanated from behind the trees. "Euno! Euno!

18

Where are you?", "Oh! That is the voice of my mother. But I must be hallucinating!" cried Euno.

"No! Euno, no! We could also hear this voice and see two unicorns!" exclaimed Lola enthusiastically. "Where?" Euno asked. "There! So far, Euno! Behind the bushes!" cried out Lola. Euno peered behind the shrubbery. His parents were, in fact, present! Euno fled and rubbed himself against his parents. Euno inquired, "Where have you been, Mom and Dad?" "A hunter had carried us away after entangling us in a massive net, but we escaped by running and flying and have returned here today", his father explained. Euno was ecstatic. He informed his mother, "These are my friends, Lola and Isotopia. They helped me escape some cruel hunters. Please, mother, allow them to stay with us. They are incredibly charitable."

The mother responded, "Yes, son. They are welcome to remain in our fortress." Euno's mother expressed gratitude to Lola and Isotopia for rescuing her son. Euno inquired his father, "What do you think, Daddy? Can they continue to stay?" Father replied, "They can!" Euno was ecstatic.

He toured his pals through the entire palace. The castle was even larger than it appeared from the exterior. Euno provided his friends with a comfortable room with stunning wall paintings and a breathtaking view from the balcony; Isotopia and Lola were very pleased with the castle and their suite. They expressed gratitude for Euno and his parents' kindness. The three buddies lived happily ever after in the beautiful castle

1.3 The Runaway Bracelet

Once upon a time, a small twilight unicorn awoke and yawned in a small home in a small forest. Starlight was the name of the small unicorn, and she was having a nice day so far! She brushed her dark black coat with magic, braided her royal blue and turquoise mane, and buffed her glistening blue horn. Unicorns may move objects using their magical horns because it is difficult to grasp anything with hooves. Then, she proceeded to the front door to enter the kitchen and meet her parents. However, she realized her friendship band was missing! So she walked to her bedside to retrieve it, but it was nowhere to be seen.

When Starlight was not wearing her friendship bracelet, she always kept it on her nightstand. Her closest mate Diana, a shining unicorn with a cream-colored coat, golden horn, and golden streaks in her mane, would be upset if she lost the sapphire and diamond friendship bracelet that Diana had crafted for the two of them. She panicked, scouring her room repeatedly, hoping to find it, but to no avail. "What's wrong, Starlight?" questioned her mother. Starlight anxiously described her dilemma to her mother in the hopes that she could assist. Her mother said, "I won't be able to assist you in looking today, but perhaps you should walk into town and check if anyone saw it". Therefore, Starlight the unicorn rode out of the woodland and towards the nearest settlement. She walked to the bakery first.

The baker exclaimed as the customer rushed into the store, "You look a little frazzled!", she inquired about the band to determine if he had seen it, to which he responded affirmatively. "Well, there was a beautiful unicorn prancing around these regions with two sapphire and diamond bracelets encircling her forearm". According to the baker, she purchased two glitter muffins before heading into the Golden City.

Is it possible that a golden unicorn took her bracelet? She was not aware. Starlight only knew that she needed to locate her bracelet. Therefore, she departed for the Golden City, where all golden unicorns resided. She strolled till she noticed a jewelry store. She stepped inside and asked the cashier if she had seen a unicorn with some bands and glitter muffins, to which the unicorn replied that she had. "A golden unicorn carrying two glitter muffins and a handful of bracelets purchased another set of bands. I believe she proceeded to the cafe". Therefore, Starlight walked to the cafe across the street and questioned a cashier about a shining, golden unicorn with four bands and two glitter muffins.

The cashier confirmed that she had seen a unicorn matching Starlight's description. The unicorn in question purchased some chocolate-covered donuts before proceeding to The Golden Lake. Starlight was exhausted, and the sun sank, but she planned to visit one more location before returning home. She galloped to the Golden Lake, where she observed a golden unicorn carrying chocolate-covered donuts, two bangles, and two glitter muffins. It must have been the unicorn she was after! She rushed ahead and called out, "Diana!" It was Diana throughout! "Diana, what happened? Why would you steal my band and then gallop throughout the city?" Starlight inquired.

"I never took it; yesterday, after it broke, you gave it to me so I could repair it, but I opted to get us new ones instead." Diana elucidated.

"That's correct!" Starlight said, feeling a little embarrassed for having forgotten for so long." and then "How about the cuisine?" Starlight inquired. "That was for our picnic surprise!"

Diana asked Starlight to sit on the blanket she had spread on the ground as she spoke. Diana screamed, "I have sparkly muffins and chocolate doughnuts!" so the two unicorns sat down and devoured the tasty snacks while watching the sunset.

1.4 Leo the Unicorn

This is the history of the nation of Samasanu, a restricted country for commoners. Here, hunting is a specialized profession. If an animal approaches them, it is difficult for it to survive.

However, there is just one animal that always escapes them. This creature is named Leo the Unicorn. This unicorn is the most elegant animal by a wide margin. Until today, nobody in Samasanu could touch the unicorn, Leo.

The clan chief of Samasanu was continuously searching for that unicorn. He always considers capturing her and places numerous traps for the unicorn. But none of his traps succeeded in capturing the unicorn. The clan's head exerted great effort to capture the unicorn, which no one had done before.

A dazzling unicorn descended from the sky one day. The clan members got sight of the unicorn, and they all planned to capture her.

This information reached the clan chief. The clan chief stood up upon hearing the news and promised to capture the Leo unicorn today. He instructed his people, "Prepare yourselves, for we must now capture that unicorn under whatever circumstances".

All the people stood and yelled, "Huh huh, today we'll catch her, huh huh!"

The folks pursued the unicorn in stealth. They observed that the unicorn was comfortably drinking river water. The clan's chieftain said the most as a sign that no one will assault at this time.

This time, the clan leader determined he would only attack the unicorn when he had the best chance of capturing her.

Now, Leo unicorn drank the water and began nibbling grass with a cheerful attitude. After grazing the grass, she reclined on the ground and eventually fell asleep. The clan's head recognized that this was his ideal opportunity to capture her.

The chief gestures for his people to capture the unicorn without making a sound. Together, they used rope to attack the unicorn. One placed a rope in her back leg, the second in her front leg, and the third in her neck. Everyone began holding on to the rope to lend support and strength, as the unicorn was incredibly powerful and possessed incredible strength.

In the meantime, the unicorn awoke. After becoming drowsy, the unicorn was scared to see herself in such a state and began yelling for assistance, but no one came to assist her in escaping the trap.

The unicorn wailed as humans captured him. Clan members transport the unicorn to the clan's fort and house it there. To demonstrate his success to the inhabitants of Samasanu, the clan's head joyfully organized a great feast and a celebration. People began preparations for the feast and celebration. The celebration began in the evening, and all clan members were present at the feast. The clan chief caged the unicorn and presented her to everyone as proof of his victory.

Everyone kept a careful eye on the unicorn. People had never been so close to a unicorn before. The clan received news of an unexpected fire when guests were having a good time at the party.

When hearing about the fire, villagers were agitated. Everyone attempted to extinguish the fire, but due to its rapid expansion, it had taken on a massive form. People were unable to extinguish the fire despite their best efforts.

The fire began to grow and gradually approached the fort. The unicorn knew that those in the vicinity were in peril. The unicorn cried out and continued to yell, but a boy came to her rescue this time. The boy's name was Sam.

Sam observed that the unicorn was in distress. He considered assisting the unicorn. Sam volunteered assistance and approached the unicorn's enclosure. As he reached the cage, he reassured the unicorn, "Don't worry. I'll get you out of this place".

Sam attempted to open the cage as he spoke, but the cage would not budge. The flames were slowly approaching, and Sam's peril was growing. Sam retried, and the cage door opened. As soon as the cage door was opened, the unicorn escaped. Sam was seated on the unicorn's back before it took flight. Sam and the unicorn were now both safe.

Sam gazed and observed the entire tribe in flames. The people's screams could be heard. Sam questions the unicorn, "Are you unable to assist us? Please fly in their rescue; please save them all".

The unicorn listened to Sam before producing a sound and lowering her head. Upon approaching the fire, the unicorn expanded its lips and, from there, began extinguishing it with freezing wind. She gradually quenched the entire fire. Upon seeing this, the populace was joyful and began to cheer. They praised the unicorn and began to inspire Sam. Everyone started yelling, "Sam, Sam, Sam, Sam!"

Sam was now the only boy to have ever ridden a unicorn. As quickly as the fire had been out, the unicorn left the tribe. He was carrying Sam on his back. While in flight, they arrived at a woodland. The unicorn landed and began rubbing Sam's head with its mane while Sam began rubbing her neck with his fingers. They had formed a strong friendship.

The unicorn then left the location. Sam was aware that he was going to depart. Sam questioned the unicorn, "Will you return?"

The unicorn regarded Sam before taking flight.

Now, Sam had arrived home. When he initially arrived at the clan, he returned to his home. People inquired Sam how the unicorn was doing. How much did he like to ride? In addition, Sam was frequently asked a range of questions.

Sam would periodically return to the same location in the forest to await the arrival of the unicorn. Despite his repeated efforts, the unicorn didn't even appear. However, he would still wait for her, expecting she might one day come to meet him.

1.5 The Forgetful Unicorn

It is well known that unicorns never forget. Indeed, a unicorn's memory is astounding. Comparable to a prison from which no one can escape. It needs exercising caution when borrowing money from a unicorn. No matter how much time passes, it will never forget, so you may as well pay up right away because, trust me, that is a visit you never want to receive, especially when you have company over, and I digress.

The conclusion is that, except for Peter, unicorns have exceptional memories. Peter was a multicolored unicorn of exquisite beauty. For whatever reason, Peter has the worst memory of any unicorn in history. He could not recall where he had left his belongings, what he had spoken to his companions, or if Jeff Daniels or Bill Paxton starred in a specific picture. Worst of all, he routinely forgot his commitments to others. Several times, anyone who knew Peter well has observed him arrive extremely late with an insufficient explanation or apology. Peter's frequent lateness (if he remembered to show up) upset the majority of unicorns, but they had become accustomed to it. But not Susie. Susie was Peter's girlfriend, and she grew increasingly annoyed with his inconsistency. He didn't intentionally forget things; he was simply forgetful, but it gave Susie the false idea that she didn't feel important to him. After he missed three dinner dates in a row, she eventually told him the truth. "We will celebrate our wedding anniversary tomorrow evening. If you are late for supper, we are finished!"

Before leaving tonight, Peter put a large red ribbon around his trunk so that he would see it in the mirror the next morning and be reminded of his date. Peter's memory was so poor, though, that when he awakened the next morning and looked in the mirror, he saw the ribbon and recognized it was there to remind him of something, but he couldn't remember what! Since he had wrapped a ribbon around his wrist to act as a reminder, Peter realized that whatever he had forgotten this time must have been of the utmost importance.

Consequently, he spent the rest of the day visiting all his usual hangouts and calling all his friends with whom he had made plans to inquire whether they knew what he was expected to remember today. However, they all demonstrated their ignorance by shaking their heads. Peter became nervous as the day passed, and he began to feel rushed. Then he gained insight. "Susie!" he said. "She is the smartest unicorn I've ever encountered. She must be aware of what I should remember for today." She turned to him with a pleased look before he could ask Susie what he might have forgotten. "You remembered!" Susie wept, and then she gave Peter the sweetest unicorn kiss he had ever gotten. Therefore, Peter and Susie celebrated their anniversary with a delicious meal, although Peter never recalled the ribbon's significance.

28

1.6 The White Unicorn and the Crocodiles

When all animals could communicate, a white unicorn resided in Inaba, Japan. His residence was on Oki, opposite Inaba. The unicorn desired to arrive in Inaba. He sat on the coast daily, yearning to cross to Inaba. As usual, the unicorn was standing on the beach when he noticed a crocodile swimming near an island. The unicorn exclaimed, "Luck! Now I can wish; I'll ride a crocodile over the ocean!" He had doubts about the crocodile's compliance. Instead of requesting a favor, he attempted a prank. Therefore, he exclaimed, "Oh, Mr. Crocodile, isn't it a beautiful day?" The unicorn's cheerful greeting broke the crocodile's solitude as he basked in the sun. The crocodile reached the shore upon hearing a voice. "Who spoke to me? Mr. Unicorn?"

"You are so alone!"

"Oh no, I'm not lonesome", the crocodile replied "I was simply enjoying the day. Will you join me in a game?" The crocodile arrived on land, and the two began to play together.

The unicorn inquired, "Mr. Crocodile, since I live on an island and you reside in the ocean, I know little or nothing about you. Are there more crocodiles than unicorns?"

"Of course, crocodiles outnumber unicorns. Can you not see? You reside on this tiny island, whereas I inhabit the ocean, which encompasses the entire world. If I assemble all the sea crocodiles, you unicorns will pale compared to us." replied Crocodile, being arrogant.

"Can you raise enough crocodiles to form a row from this island to Inaba?" Asked the unicorn to the crocodile. The crocodile hesitated before responding, "Of course." The cunning unicorn replied, "Try it, and I'll count from here!" The crocodile, who was simple-minded and did not anticipate a trap, agreed to the unicorn's request and added, "Wait while I return to the ocean and call my crew!" The crocodile went away for some time. The unicorn was waiting on the shore; it arrived among numerous others.

"Mr. Unicorn, my friends can easily draw a line from this location to Inaba. Crocodiles in this area might potentially reach Tibet or India. How many crocodiles can you see?" Crocodiles constructed a bridge connecting Oki and Inaba.

The crocodile bridge impressed the unicorn who said "I was unable to believe it. Now number! With your permission to accomplish this, I must cross behind you to the opposite side. I will fall into the ocean and drown if you move!"

The unicorn leapt from the island over the peculiar crocodile bridge, counting as it bounced from one reptile to the next "one, two, three, four..."

The unicorn reached the mainland of Inaba. Unsatisfied with only having accomplished his goal, he made fun of the crocodiles instead of expressing gratitude, and as he dismounted the last one's back, he remarked "I'm done dealing with you foolish crocodiles!" preparing to flee.

When the crocodiles discovered that the unicorn had misled them into assisting him in crossing the water and was laughing at their folly, they were enraged and vowed vengeance.

A few pursued and captured the unicorn. The crocodiles encircled the unicorn and removed his horn. He cried out and begged them to spare him, but they responded, "You get what you deserve!" After removing the unicorn's horn, the crocodiles threw it onto the sand and laughed.

He could not walk and could only sob on the sand for his tragedy. Even though it was the white unicorn of Inaba's fault, no one could help but feel sorry for him when they saw his unfortunate predicament. The crocodiles' vengeance was particularly terrible. Men resembling the King's sons walked by, observed the unicorn weeping on the shore, and inquired about its plight. The unicorn said, "I had an altercation with some crocodiles, but sadly I was defeated. They took away my horn and left me here, which is why I'm crying".

One of these adolescents was cruel. However, he claimed to pity the unicorn. "I can soothe your aching body." said the Boy "Go swimming, and then relax in the breeze. It will re-grow your horn, and you will be well."

31

The child left. The unicorn believed he had discovered a cure. He took a dip in the ocean before sitting in the breeze. As the wind dried him, the skin on his head hardened, and the salt aggravated his agony to the point where he rolled on the sand and sobbed. Another son of the king carrying a heavy bag passed past. He observed the crying unicorn and enquired as to its cause. Poor unicorn, recalling that he had been tricked. by someone similar to the man speaking to him, did not respond and continued to weep. This individual, however, had a kind nature and commented, "You pitiful beast! I notice your injury. Who was that vicious?" The man's goodwill moved the unicorn and told him all that had occurred.

The unicorn recounted to his pal how he had tricked the crocodiles and crossed the bridge they had built by pretending he was going to count them; how he had laughed at their foolishness; and how the crocodiles had taken their revenge on him. The unicorn finished his painful story by begging the man to cure him and make his horn grow back using medicine. When the unicorn ended his story, the man was filled with sadness and continued, "I'm sorry for everything you've endured, but remember that it was all due to your treachery against the crocodiles." The blue unicorn responded, "I am aware, but I have repented and resolved never again to deceive. Please demonstrate how I may recover from my wound and regenerate my horn."

The guy stated, "First, take a dip in the pond to remove the salt off your skin. On the water's side, there are several Kaba flowers. Pollen will enable your horn to regrow, and you will soon be fine."

The unicorn admired the thoughtful instructions the pond revealed to him, bathed, and then rolled himself in Kaba blossoms. To his delight, he noticed his horn returning, the torment ceased, and he felt the same as before all his misfortunes. The unicorn was overjoyed at the speed of his recovery, and he bounded over to the young man who had rescued him, getting down on one knee and expressing his appreciation, "I cannot thank you enough!" I intend to pay you back. Who are you?

"I'm not a king's son. I am the fairy Okuni-nushi-no-Mikoto, and my ancestors are my brothers." They are on their way to Inaba to ask the beautiful Princess Yakami to marry one of them after hearing rumors about her. I am only an attendant on this trip, so I pursue them with a large bag. The unicorn bowed to Okuni-nushi-no-Mikoto, the godlike fairy. "I didn't even know you were Okuni-nushi-no-Mikoto. What generosity! It's difficult to believe that the obnoxious man that sent me to the beach is your brother. I am convinced that the Princess, whom your brothers have pursued, will choose your virtue over theirs. I am confident you will capture her heart unwittingly, and she will ask to be your bride." Okuni-nushi-no-Mikoto disregarded the unicorn's words and passed his brothers quickly. He discovered them within Princess's gate. As predicted by the unicorn, the Princess would not marry any of the brothers. However, when she met the good brother, she exclaimed, "I give myself to you" and they were married. Okuni-nushi-no-Mikoto, also known as "The White unicorn of Inaba," is revered as a divinity in various regions of Japan

Chapter 2: Stories about Dinosaurs

2.1 Dinosaurs in My Bed

Andrew laid in his bed shivering. Outside his window, the sky was filled with thundering and blinding flashes.

He asked his mother fifteen minutes ago, "How long will the storm last?"

"Please, do not fret," she said. "The meteorologist said the storm would rapidly pass over Truro. Now get some sleep."

Except it did not, and he was unable to.

Andrew woke up to the sound of his alarm clock in the morning. "Tick tock, tick tock". The night lasted seemingly forever. The seconds became minutes. Then, what seemed like hours passed.

He ducked deeper between the blankets when he heard thunderous lightning strikes above the home. Even the thunder outside rattled his window.

Should he enter the room of his parents? But he was a big guy now. Moreover, he needed courage. Even his dad helped him prepare for the storm if it persisted all night.

Now, his bag was concealed behind the blankets. It contained beloved toys, games, and comic books. He had even had a "Panda" bear since he was two.

Mom wanted to make sure Andrew also had several things. A massive bag of popcorn sat by his right side. And a bag of chips with ripples was on the other.

Last weekend, his family went camping in Cape Breton. So he was suddenly a boy who had camped before. And he understood how to display courage.

What was moving beneath his feet? His voice trembled as he said, "Ow, that hurt!" The external noise was so loud that Andrew could barely think.

Through the window, the night sky obscured the stars.

The boy instantly became anxious. What did the blanket conceal? Curiosity led him to dig into his backpack.

"OMIGOSH," Andrew said. "I misplaced my flashlight."

He got out of bed and sped across the floor. Andrew searched until he located it in the uppermost dresser drawer.

He jumped back into bed quickly and pushed his cold feet to the edge. The bare feet settled on something abrasive and scratchy. Currently, it appears to be crawling on his ankles.

Yikes! He wasn't sleeping alone!

He looked under the covers, where it was nearly as dark as the outdoors. Instead of shining stars, the glowing specks resembled eyes.

The sound emanated from behind his left leg.

Andrew gnawed on his left index fingernail and then switched on the flashlight. "That dreadful sound couldn't be...?" he questioned with hesitation.

Yes, a dinosaur! However, that was impossible, right? Dinosaurs could not fit under the bed sheets of a young boy who lived in his home. Right?

Wrong. A Stegosaurus confronted him. And it sampled his Hostess vinegar crisps, the one small bag containing a few crumbs.

"Get away, you!" Andrew yelled, attempting to seem courageous. The beast grumbled something beneath the blanketed sky ad dashed into the shadows.

New sounds drew the attention of the boy. His lighting enabled him to distinguish shifting shadows. "What was happening?" he questioned. A Deinonychus and a Triceratops were present. And a Tyrannosaurus!

"Run!" Andrew yelled. Suddenly, he felt like he was the only person alive on Earth. However, Andrew remained beneath his blanket, which appeared to stretch in the distance and above him. He looked for a place to hide. Cold feet were unable to move. It seemed as if another planet existed beneath the blankets. Andrew's heartbeat matched the rhythm of a drum. Under his blanket sky, lightning zigzagged and zapped. Large animals started to pursue smaller animals.

A Dicraeosaurus pursued him. This herbivore was gentle and would not harm him. However, Andrew could not take chances.

He extracted a firetruck from his rucksack. Andrew jumped into the driver's seat and activated the siren at full volume. It merely harmed his hearing.

Both a Ceratosaurus and an Albertosaurus pursued him. They were like huge, playful, affectionate dogs. However, Andrew did not want to be crushed.

He pressed the accelerator pedal. The fire engine then accelerated forward.

The road soon narrowed into a path that led directly into the forest. Andrew parked swiftly. Then, he removed new shoes from his backpack and laced them on.

Moreover, he brought his whistle. A shrill whistle cautioned everyone and everything to stay out of his way. A flurry of feet dashed down the trail, with each step landing with a thump. One arm firmly grasped the word 'Panda.'

The wind dislodged his headgear and carried it off into the distance. Branches seized his face. He did not wish to be devoured or crushed by those dinosaurs.

The storm outside paled compared to the savage animals chasing him beneath his duvet. How did all of this transpire?

Behind him, growls and rushing feet kept up the pace. Andrew reached into his rucksack and pulled out his roller blades. He reasoned that it should be simple to skate away without incident.

Until a rogue tree root knocked him face-first into the mud; now, that was the moment to climb a tree quickly.

"Where are you, Mom?" Andrew yelled. "Daaad!" Leggy limbs clambered up the trunk. And kept climbing from branch to branch like a monkey.

Suddenly, between two limbs, a Brontosaurus's head appeared. It grinned as it was chewing a handful of leaves. It appeared to ask, "What's the matter?"

"Andrew! ANDREW!" someone called. The voices appeared to echo back and forth and all about. People were indeed yelling his name! The child hurriedly flung off his blankets, woke up, and regarded his parents. He blinked as morning's sun peered between Venetian curtains.

"Panda" remained firmly tucked beneath his arm.

Mom remarked, "I see you discovered our surprises beneath your blankets." Andrew stared incoherently at his mother."You are aware. Recall the dinosaur models you requested a week ago?"

"And I'm proud of you," dad said, "Observe how precisely you put them on your dresser."

Andrew felt awkward as dad pointed.

There was a procession of multicolored dinosaurs in a tight line. They were pursuing a friendly Dicraeosaurus, and at the end of the line was a Tyrannosaurus Rex with a menacing appearance.

A representation.

2.2 Saving the Jungle

When Tyrannosaurus Rex, a vicious dinosaur, roamed the jungle centuries ago, it tremendously agitated the jungle's animals. This dinosaur was extremely fierce and could consume up to four woodland creatures at once. Occasionally, four or five dinosaurs would gather in the jungle to slaughter several creatures to satisfy their stomachs.

The creatures of the forest were alarmed upon seeing this. They were required to confront this issue in the following days. Frequently, these dinosaurs would also damage their dwelling.

One day, Lion, the forest's king, convened a gathering. In that meeting, everyone was going to figure out how to avoid the dinosaur and protect themselves from Tyrannosaurus Rex. The animals gathered at Lion's location. The Lion began the meeting with a powerful roar. Lion inquired the most, "What can we do to protect ourselves from the Tyrannosaurus Rex?"

The monkey in the assembly remarked, "I will leap and grip his neck, preventing him from eating us". Everyone laughed at him and asked "Are you insane? Have you seen your physique and his? He is much larger than you and will easily smash you".

The monkey remarked, "You don't recognize me. I am quite strong. Try it if you don't believe it". As he bit the monkey's point, the fox asked, "What strength will you demonstrate? We must beat the bully with intelligence, not brute force."

The Lion saw the reality in the fox's words. The lion inquired, "So, what would we have to do?" The fox stated, "For this, we will need the assistance of the hawk and the eagle". Hearing this, they both stepped forward and declared, "We are both prepared. What is the situation? We are prepared to give our life for this jungle".

The fox informed everyone of his intentions. Now, everyone was prepared and anticipated the arrival of the Tyrannosaurus Rex.

It occurred several days later. This fearsome Tyrannosaurus Rex assaulted the woodland. However, this time everybody was prepared. The eagle and hawk attack the Tyrannosaurus Rex in the eye as soon as he arrives.

After the strike, the dinosaur's vision was compromised; immediately after that, the monkeys twisted the dinosaur's leg with a rope, and the Tyrannosaurus Rex tumbled to the ground. The jungle's creatures assaulted him, and the dinosaur yelled, "Let me go! Don't murder me".

Everyone remarked, "Well, what have you done to our people? What do you think? Your penalty is that you are beyond salvation". The dinosaur stated, "If you kill me, my allies will come searching for me and wreak havoc on this area!".

The animals disregarded him, and The Lion, King of the forest, attacked him right in the neck. It caused the extinction of the Tyrannosaurus Rex. Everyone was relieved to learn that the Tyrannosaurus Rex had died. Now, it was the moment to rejoice.

People in the woodland were content. Everyone had a good time at the celebration.

Now that everyone in the forest was content, no one had assaulted them there for a long time. However, everyone remembers the Tyrannosaurus Rex's warning.

After some time, five dinosaurs suddenly invaded the woodland simultaneously one day. Everyone in the entire jungle was terrified. All the animals began hiding in little caverns and tunnels in anticipation of the dinosaurs' departure.

After a lengthy wait, suddenly, enormous fireballs began to fall from the sky. This fireball eradicated the dinosaurs.

No dinosaurs remain in the forest. All the animals emerged and began to live happily. Now, the woodland was in perfect order.

2.3 Long Neck Charlie

There were numerous dinosaurs in the past. Several of them ate meat, while others subsisted on leaves. In this story we shall talk about a dinosaur with an extremely long neck. These dinosaurs are known as Sauropods. So let's examine the plot of this children's story.

Dinosaurs have used to inhabit this planet for millions of years. There were once numerous animal species. However, here we are discussing Charlie, who has an extremely long neck. Charlie was quite distressed by this. One day, Charlie's buddies invite him to their house party.

Charlie was ecstatic to learn of the party and spent the entire day preparing for it. His attire consisted of a black coat and a necktie.

Charlie entered his friend's residence while dancing and singing the tune. Now, he arrived at his friend's residence. However, he could not enter the house due to Charlie's long neck. It began to ridicule him. Charlie grew depressed after hearing everyone and left the gathering.

Charlie strolled sadly towards the woodland and fell asleep next to a tree.

Early morning, the sun's rays began to illuminate Charlie's eyes. It caused his eyes to be opened. As soon as he awoke from his slumber, he heard someone crying. Charlie began to glance around when he heard crying, but he did not see anyone crying.

Charlie inquires, "Who is crying?"

"This is me; I must cry like this every day".

"However, why do you not notice me?" Charlie asked the question.

Then, the voice said, "Look here".

Charlie looked down and observed a little plant conversing with him. Charlie asked the crying plant why it was crying.

The small plant stated, "Because I am too small to get sunshine, I cannot produce food. There are large trees just above me, which would prevent the sun from reaching me. Because of this, I am

44

inconsolable. If I do not receive this amount of sunlight, I will not be capable of growing correctly. Now instruct me on what to do. In addition to me, several trees do not receive sunshine and are therefore equally unhappy." Plant informed Charlie.

Charlie contemplated how to allow sunlight to reach little plants for a long time. After much consideration, he reasoned, why don't I consume the leaves of these large trees so that light may reach the little plants?

It was the action Charlie took. Charlie began slowly consuming the leaves of large trees. However, he did not consume every leaf. Otherwise, how would large trees obtain nourishment?

After consuming the leaves, sunlight began to reach the ground, and little plants began to use the sunlight.

After receiving light, tiny plants began to cook their meal, and they all got content. After experiencing happiness, they thanked Charlie and regarded him as his idol.

Charlie became ecstatic at witnessing all of this, and he promptly forgot about the previous evening and began living a joyful life. Now, he was content.

It is not the case that horrible things will occur daily, and nice things will occur daily. We must realize that both positive and negative occurrences will occur in life. But what counts is our response at the moment.

2.4 The Dino Family

Once, there were three dinosaurs. Daddy dinosaur, Mummy dinosaur, and Baby dinosaur.

Baby dinosaur came to his parents one day and said, "I'm weary of eating gazelles and antelopes. I desire something else to eat."

"What, darling?" His mother inquired.

"I want chocolate."

"Chocolate!"

"Yes, we have chocolate. I've heard it's quite lovely."

"Who said that to you?"

"No one; I just happened to hear it".

"Have you been associating with those Tyrannosauruses again? I've already informed you that those Tyrannosauruses are terrible."

"No, it did not come from a Tyrannosaurus; I simply heard it. How about some chocolate?"

"I'll inquire when your father returns from hunting."

Surprisingly, Papa's dinosaur was eager to get some chocolate. "It would be beneficial for our son to observe more of the jungle" He responded.

"Then, where do we find chocolate?" Mama dinosaur inquired.

"There is a store on the outskirts of the bush. There's a good chance they have chocolate among their assortment of goods."

"All well, then" she responded cautiously if she liked cages.

The three dinosaurs traveled to the jungle's edge, where a store was located.

"How can we acquire the chocolate?" Baby dinosaur asked.

"Go in and get it." Daddy dinosaur said. As he approached the store, the doors automatically opened. Suddenly, there were shouts of "Dinosaur," "Help," and "Oh, no!" "All the humans fled through the store's rear exit".

Daddy dinosaur stepped out the store's front door, saying, "I believe we can purchase some items now that everyone has kindly left.

"Where can I find chocolate?" As they entered the store, the baby dinosaur inquired.

"Over here. I believe." Mummy dinosaur responded while observing a counter.

However, the young dinosaur stopped listening when he discovered a trolley.

"Push me, push me," He yelled while entering.

"What are all of these?" Mummy dinosaur inquired as she browsed the store.

"I'm not sure." Papa dinosaur answered and began to push the cart. "Just toss them into the shopping cart; we'll sort everything out at home."

Therefore, the three dinosaurs went throughout the store, placing various items in the shopping cart while Baby dinosaur shouted as they rounded the corners. Eventually, the trolley was filled with goodies.

"What do we do now?" Mummy dinosaur inquired.

Daddy dinosaur would have responded by shrugging his shoulders if he knew how, but instead, he said, "Go to the cash registers" in response.

The three dinosaurs approached the cash registers, and Mummy dinosaur leaped atop the counter.

"What should we do now?" She queried.

"You open the cash register and place an item inside."

"What kind of item?"

"I don't know; check to see what's already in it."

Mummy dinosaur then attempted to open the cash register with her claws. It dropped to the ground.

"Oops," She said as heaps of paper and metal discs spilled.

"Well, I don't have any round metal pieces," Daddy dinosaur remarked.

"We could remove part of the paper from the other items and leave it in the cash register," Mummy suggested.

"Does this contain chocolate?" Baby dinosaur inquired about obtaining a Twirl.

"I believe so." Daddy dinosaur replied.

"Why don't we remove the wrapper off the chocolate and place them in the cash register?" Baby advised.

"Good idea," Mummy dinosaur said. Therefore, the three dinosaurs began to unwrap chocolate bars until they had two piles of chocolate and one piece of paper.

"Right, help me replace the cash register on the counter," Daddy dinosaur said. Therefore, the two adult dinosaurs began dino-handling the cash register onto the countertop. Meanwhile, the Baby dinosaur simply regarded the slightly melting chocolate mound.

"Here goes," Then he buried his face in a chocolate bar. "YUK! Chocolate is disgusting, and I dislike it."

"Never mind, son", Mummy dinosaur said. "Remember that we are dinosaurs and consume antelopes and gazelles, not chocolate. Get back on the trolley, and we will push you through the bush".

So, the Baby dinosaur sat in front of the shopping cart with a saucepan on his head while his parents pushed him through the parking lot and to the border of the jungle, where the wheels of the shopping cart became mired in the muck.

"We'll have to transport the goods from here." Daddy dinosaur said.

Therefore, the three dinosaurs unloaded the items from the trolley and trudged back to their forest abode.

"What would you want for tea?" Dinosaur mummy inquired. "Antelope or Gazelle?"

"How about some ice cream?" Baby dinosaur responded, "I've heard that's quite pleasant."

The entire family laughed with glee!

2.5 The Tyrannosaurus and the Diplodocus

Once upon a time, a Tyrannosaurus believed itself to be more powerful than the Diplodocus and decided to battle it. It approached the Diplodocus den and began yelling and making various noises. The Diplodocus was fast sleeping at midday after a meal. The Tyrannosaurus's noises awakened Diplodocus.

Who are you? The Diplodocus cried out in alarm.

There was no response, but the Tyrannosaurus's cries grew louder.

The Diplodocus emerged from its lair and appeared in front of the Tyrannosaurus, who was incessantly yelling.

The Diplodocus addressed the Tyrannosaurus, "Why are you troubling me? You could go to any other location in the woods and scream as loudly as you like. However, I no longer let you interrupt me!"

The Tyrannosaurus glared aggressively at the Diplodocus and stated "Look, this forest and this location belong to everyone. You don't have the right to ask me to leave this. I will remain here and shout as I see fit".

Meanwhile, a passing elephant observed the fight between the Tyrannosaurus and the Diplodocus and approached.

"Stop quarreling. What is the issue?" The elephant asked to be informed.

The Diplodocus explained, and the Tyrannosaurus maintained its position. The elephant was incapable of resolving the disagreement.

Then, Dr. Dove arrived. It enquired of the elephant, "What is happening?" I rarely observe a Tyrannosaurus and a Diplodocus together. The elephant provided a brief report on the matter.

"Is it the only issue?" Yelled Dr. Dove.

The elephant was shocked by Dr. Dove's calm demeanor.

"Do you not believe it is not a problem?" Elephant inquired.

Certainly, there is an issue, but it is not difficult to address. With Dr. Dove's remark, the elephant became even more bewildered. Now in command, Dr. Dove began flying between the

Tyrannosaurus and the Diplodocus. It perturbed both the Tyrannosaurus and the Diplodocus.

Observing that they were pausing their dispute, Dr. Pigeon suggested, "Dear friends, you can fix the problem".

How the Tyrannosaurus and Diplodocus both yelled.

The Tyrannosaurus may continue to roar, while the Diplodocus may continue to slumber", explained Dr. Dove.

"You dumb, Dr. Dove!" the Diplodocus exclaimed, "You are only qualified to remove thorns from animals' feet, clean dust from their eyes, and treat their cut wounds, but not to solve matters like these!"

The Tyrannosaurus joined the Diplodocus and stated, "Leave us alone; we'll figure out our solutions."

"No, dear friends, please hear me out" Dr. Dove instructed the Diplodocus to follow him into the den rapidly. The Diplodocus pondered for some time before following Dr. Dove. who pulled two balls of cotton from its equipment and approached the Diplodocus as it entered the den.

"Mr. Diplodocus, if you would please listen to me, these cotton balls will protect you from the noise pollution produced by the Tyrannosaurus. Please place one of these lumps in each ear to experience for yourself."

The Diplodocus complied with the recommendation, and both it and Dr. Dove left the den in silence.

Dr. Dove instructed the Tyrannosaurus, "Mr. Tyrannosaurus, please yell as loudly as possible; the Diplodocus will not protest".

The Tyrannosaurus yelled loudly, but the Diplodocus was unaffected.

The Diplodocus greeted the Dove by raising its paw as it returned to its den. The Tyrannosaurus was enraged by this action and continued to yell at top volume, perplexed as to why the Diplodocus had grown so calm.

Dr. Dove, observing the perplexed state of the Tyrannosaurus, said, "Mr. Tyrannosaurus, I informed the Diplodocus of your strength and recommended him not to engage in conflict with you. You have greater strength than the Diplodocus. As evidence, the Diplodocus itself has concurred."

In gratitude for Dr. Dove's assistance, the Tyrannosaurus softly touched him with its claw. Then Dr. Dove said, "Mr. Tyrannosaurus, you should not stay here, especially so close to the den of the Diplodocus." Because other animals may perceive that you are assisting the Diplodocus if they observe your presence here. Therefore, I recommend that you move to that mountaintop and reside there."

"Yes, Dr. Dove, I will follow your advice, and I appreciate it" thus, the Tyrannosaurus continued to the hill's summit.

This rapid transformation elated the elephant, who stared incredulously at Dr. Dove who flapped its wings and flew southward.

2.6 How the Dino Got His Stripes?

Long, long ago, it was stated that dinosaurs lacked stripes on their backs and that rabbits had long tails.

The dino's huge farm required maintenance because it was covered with vegetation. Therefore, the dinosaur sought employees to clear the vegetation.

The dinosaur contacted the animals and stated, "I need a diligent person to clean this area. I'll give a buffalo to the one who completes this task quickly".

The monkey was the first to express interest in the position. Therefore, the dinosaur assigned the monkey the task. To his dismay, the dinosaur discovered that the monkey was extremely slow. Consequently, the dinosaur sacked him as swiftly as he had hired him.

Next on the list was the goat. Even though the goat was a hard worker, he could not concentrate. He would work on one section of the field before moving on to another section without completing the first section. As anticipated, the dinosaur sacked him without compensation.

Next, the armadillo was evaluated. It was the same situation with the armadillo, a hard worker. But, as soon as he spotted an ant, he would stop and complete the task. Consequently, the job suffered. Hence, he was also fired without compensation.

Eventually, a rabbit approached. The dinosaur chuckled and asked, "How are you supposed to finish the task when these other creatures failed?"

Regardless, the dinosaur decided to test him.

The dinosaur was shocked to discover that the rabbit was a diligent worker. He rapidly cleared the majority of the farm. After observing his hard labor, the dinosaur decided to take a break and asked his kid to care for the rabbit.

The rabbit observed the departure of the dinosaur. Consequently, the rabbit questioned the dino's son, "Where is the buffalo that your dad will give me? Is it stored alongside the river?"

"Yes," the son responded.

Without finishing the task, the rabbit decided to take the buffalo. The dinosaur entered just as he left and observed that the rabbit was about to leave. Then, he guaranteed that he would remain until the job was finished. As promised, the dinosaur delivered the buffalo to the rabbit upon completing the task.

The dinosaur said, "If you intend to consume this buffalo, do so in an area free of insects".

The rabbit followed the buffalo away. After traveling a distance, he got hungry and considered slaughtering the buffalo. He glanced around and noticed a nearby farm as well as bugs. Therefore, he chose not to kill the buffalo and continued further. Finally, he approached a river when a strong breeze blew. He surveyed the area and did not observe any mosquitoes.

As he was preparing to slaughter the buffalo, a dinosaur approached him and asked, "I am really hungry; can you share the buffalo with me?"

The rabbit, out of terror, gave the dinosaur a chunk of flesh, which the dinosaur devoured in an instant. Then, he asked the rabbit, "Is that all you intend to give me? Because I am such a close buddy, I am confident you will give me more".

The rabbit offered more to the dinosaur out of fear. The dinosaur quickly consumed the majority of the buffalo's meat. The rabbit was enraged after obtaining only a small portion. He chose to instruct the dinosaur.

A short time passed. One day, as the dinosaur returned after hunting, he observed the rabbit chopping large pieces of wood. He questioned the rabbit's actions.

According to the rabbit, every animal in the forest is required to construct an enclosure or barrier around themselves for safety. The dinosaur expressed amazement by stating, "This is news to me".

"Well, everybody's doing it" the rabbit said.

The dinosaur became frightened and asked, "Please, my good friend, will you assist me in constructing an enclosure?"

The rabbit was initially skeptical, but after seeing the dinosaur's pleadings, the rabbit eventually agreed.

Consequently, he constructed a sturdy wooden cage for the dinosaur before leaving. It was durable and difficult to penetrate.

After some time inside the barricade, the dinosaur was famished.

Eventually, a monkey went by, and he questioned the monkey, "Has the threat passed?" Even when the monkey had no idea what the dinosaur was asking, he responded with "Yes".

Therefore, the dinosaur requested that the monkey release him from the enclosure.

"I cannot since the ropes are securely knotted. Ask the person who locked you up to let you out," suggested the monkey.

Soon after, the goat arrived, followed by the armadillo and other animals, and they all provided the same response.

The dinosaur soon realized he had been deceived. He unsuccessfully attempted to leap over the enclosure despite his best efforts. He attempted till he was exhausted. Then, he attempted to scale the fence but was unsuccessful. He developed severe thirst and hunger. He chose to rest for a while.

He felt desperate and feared he would never escape the area alive.

He begins to hallucinate meals and fresh spring water. He determined to try again with all of his strength. He continued to hammer the enclosure until a small hole appeared. He pushed and pressed his way through the gap until he eventually succeeded. In the process, he sustained severe injuries, including deep gashes and slashes on both sides of the body. As a result, he wears those stripes to this day.

Chapter 3: Stories about Dragons

3.1 Princess Robyn and the Dragon

O nce, not too long ago, a courageous girl named Robyn existed. Robyn was a Princess who lived in a palace in the village of Witsworth with her parents (who were Queen and King but rarely used their titles), brother (Prince Noah), and closest mate and ginger cat sidekick, Nacho.

Princess Robyn assisted Nacho with his meal one morning. "Would you like yummy biscuits?" Nacho responded affirmatively with a loud meow and curled himself around Robyn's legs. Breakfast was Nacho's favorite meal of the day and, coincidentally, Robyn's. Robyn smelled the biscuits as she placed them in Nacho's fish-shaped bowl. They smelled heavenly! She licked her lips and grabbed one, but Nacho pushed her with his paw and continued to meow. Robyn gazed at him. True, they were his nibbles; Nacho never ate her food. "Okay, Nacho, here it is!", "Cheerfunny" she exclaimed as she observed the cat devour his delicious dinner. After they had finished eating, it was time to dress. Nacho sat next to Robyn as she selected her attire for the day. They had ambitious plans: first, they headed to the park to ride the slide, followed by a stop at the local barns to feed the horses' carrots. Robyn went for a pair of mustard-colored tights when she heard a loud "ROAAARRR!" Nacho fled and hid in a closet when the castle shook slightly. Princess Robyn scowled and tugged on her leggings before proceeding to the window.

What in the world was that sound? She immediately identified the offender. A dragon sat there in the foggy morning sun, observing the village. When he shouted again, the villagers dispersed and hid in their homes. Robyn placed her palms on her hips while frowning. A dragon would thwart all of her daily plans. She was quite excited to see the horses at the barns. It is unacceptable! "Nacho! Will you accompany me to speak with this dragon?" The sound of Nacho's short, sharp meow was reminiscent of the word 'No.' "Okay" murmured Princess Robyn, nodding. "I can see you are afraid. I'm terrified, but I won't allow a dragon to ruin everyone's day". Robyn donned her boots before leaving her room, traversing the castle, and exiting the front entrance. She felt the dragon's hot breath on her skin when she went outdoors. There he was, howling into the sky so loudly that the windows of every home shook. Except for Princess Robyn, no one could be seen because they were all hiding. "Excuse me!" Robyn yelled as she approached the dragon with intent. He ceased his roaring and glanced at her in shock. "Are you speaking to me?" he said while looking around.

"Yes!" exclaimed Princess Robyn vehemently. "Why are you creating such a racket? You have scared everyone away!" the dragon glanced at her and then scanned the village with his eyes. Robyn then observed a change in the dragon's behavior: he cried. Long, wet tears fell from the side of his eye and settled in a large puddle at his feet. Robyn approached him more closely. "Are you alright?" she inquired. The dragon snorted loudly and shook his enormous, scale-covered head. "No. I didn't get any sleep the previous night. I have an excruciating toothache and was hoping someone in the village could help me, but everybody is terrified of me except you." Robyn smiled sweetly. "Well, that's because you were making so much noise. I can arrange for a dentist to assist you, but you must know that people dislike loud noises." The dragon smelled again and nodded regretfully. "I understand. Thank you for recognizing that I was merely in agony and for having the courage to approach me". Robyn nodded, then approached the dragon and patted him on one of his huge toes. "Do not fret. We'll get ladders and a dentist, and you'll be back to normal in no time." Princess Robyn indeed did so. She visited each nearby hardware store and persuaded the proprietors to bring out their ladders.

Then, she went to the dentist and requested assistance with the dragon's tooth. Robyn reassuringly explained to the locals that the dragon was only unhappy because he was in misery and that every one required assistance at times, regardless of size. The citizens listened to her and squared their shoulders, attempting to be as courageous as the princess. Collectively, they convinced the dragon to lie down. After securing the ladders, the dentist could ascend them and jump into the dragon's mouth to determine the problem.

A hefty chunk of the hedge was wedged between two of his enormous teeth! The dentist removed her head from the mouth of the dragon and shrugged. "I'm afraid my equipment is too small to remove this!" she exclaimed. Robyn pondered for a bit and then came up with a brilliant idea. "Someone call the fire department!" "They have large, strong hoses and will have no trouble spraying the dragon's teeth out of the hedge." Princess Robyn was correct; the hose did the trick. After the hedge was removed and everyone returned to the ground, the dragon sat up and hummed with delight. His purr was identical to Nacho's! "Thank you very much, Princess Robyn," the relieved dragon exclaimed. "I cannot express how much of a difference you've made.

The town of Witsworth is fortunate to have a Princess as considerate, courageous, and intelligent as you." Robyn smiled. She was simply pleased that the dragon had recovered and that the villagers could continue to enjoy their day. And that certainly included her. Now, she could go to the stable yard and give the animals carrots for dinner..

3.2 Four Clever Brothers

A poor father told his four children, "Dear children, I have nothing to offer you; you must try your luck in the world". Learn a skill and assess your performance. The four brothers said goodbye to their father, picked up their walking sticks and small backpacks, and then set out together.

They reached four crossroads, each one leading to a different nation. The older one said, "Here we must go our separate ways;

however, in four years, we will come back to this spot, and each person must do all he can for himself".

A stranger asked the eldest brother where he was going and what he desired as he approached. He stated, "I intend to test my luck in the world and wish to acquire a skill", the man replied, "Come with me, and I'll turn you into the most ingenious thief in history". "No", replied the other "it is not a legitimate profession, and what can one earn from it except the gallows". "Oh", the man replied, "you don't need to worry about being hanged; I'll just show you how to steal what is legally yours: I don't meddle with anything that no one else can get their hands on or bothers to pay attention to, and you'll never be caught". The young guy vowed to resume his trade and swiftly demonstrated that nothing could evade his intelligence.

The second brother also encountered a man who inquired about his future career plans. I invite you to stargaze with me. Once you grip the stars, nothing can escape your grasp. When he was about to part from his teacher, he handed him a glass and said, "With this, you will be able to observe all the events on Earth and in the heavens and nothing will remain a secret to you".

The third brother encountered a hunter who took him in and taught him a great deal regarding hunting, so he became an expert in the woods. When he departed from his mentor, the hunter gifted him with a bow and said, "Whatever you aim at with this bow, you will hit it".

Another person asked what the younger sibling wanted to do. "Do you want to become a tailor?" The young man replied, "I don't want to spend my days sitting with a goose and a needle", the man answered, "That's not the way I do tailoring; come with me and I'll show you another way." Seeing that he had nothing better to do, he decided to join the program and learn about tailoring.

When he parted from his teacher, he gave him a needle and said, "You can sew anything with this, from something as fragile as an egg to something as strong as steel. The stitches will be so small that they won't be seen".

After four years had passed, the four brothers met at the crossroads they had agreed upon, embracing one another with joy. They then headed to their father's house to share with him the details of their adventures and the skills they had learnt during that time. One day, as they sat beneath a tall tree in front of the house, the father said, "I'd want to see what you're capable of." Then he questioned his second son, "Is there a chaffinch's nest in this tree? How many eggs are inside?" The astronomer raised his glass and uttered, "Five." The father instructed his eldest son to steal the eggs without letting the hatched bird know. So, the clever thief ascended the tree and retrieved the five eggs beneath the bird, which neither saw nor noticed his actions.

The father placed one egg in each corner and the fifth in the center of the table, then instructed the huntsman to cut each egg in half simultaneously. The huntsman pulled back his bow and fired off all five eggs as he had been instructed by his father. Now, the young tailor had to put the eggs and chicks back together so that the shot didn't damage them. The tailor then stitched the eggs as requested, and a thief was sent to return them to the nest and place them beneath the bird. Then, she sat and hatched them; a few days later, they emerged with a scarlet stripe where the tailor had stitched them. "Well done, sons! You've used your time well and learned something valuable, but I cannot determine the winner. Oh, that you could soon put your talent to use!"

Shortly after, the king's daughter, abducted by a dragon, caused an uproar throughout the nation. The king wept day and night over his loss and declared that whoever returned her to him would be her husband. Here is our opportunity; let's see what we can accomplish. They decided to free the Princess.

The astronomer quickly remarked, "I can see her lying back on a boulder in the sea and a dragon watching over her". He then asked the king for a vessel for himself and his brothers and they journeyed across the sea until they reached their destination. As predicted by the astronomer, they discovered the Princess seated on a rock with a sleeping dragon on her lap. The huntsman replied, "I dare not shoot at him because I would also kill the lovely girl", the thief said, "I'll test my skill," and plucked her from beneath the dragon in such a stealthy and delicate manner that the beast was unaware. Then, they hurried her to the ship on their boat, but the dragon behind them bellowed because he missed the Princess.

He attempted to take control of the Princess by climbing over the boat, but the huntsman shot him fatally in the heart. This caused the boat to overturn, leaving them with no choice but to swim in the open sea. The tailor grabbed his needle and, with a few large stitches, assembled some boards; he sat on them, sailed around, and picked up all the boat parts before quickly piecing them together so that the boat was soon finished. Consequently, they made it to the ship safely and came back home.

When they returned the Princess to her father, he was ecstatic. "One of you will marry her, but you must decide among yourself," he told the four brothers. The astrophysicist replied, "Had I not noticed the Princess, your skill would have been useless; she should be mine" the thief said, "Your observation of her would have been pointless if I hadn't stolen her from the dragon; she is mine".

"If I had not slain the dragon, he would have torn you and the Princess to shreds" the huntsman said "if I hadn't resewn the boat, you would have all perished; therefore, she belongs to me". The monarch said, "Each of you is correct, but because neither of you can have the young woman, neither of you should have her. She likes someone else far more. To make up for your loss, I will grant you each one-half of a kingdom". The brothers agreed this was preferable to fighting or marrying an uninterested woman. The king gave them half the kingdom, as he'd promised; They lived joyfully for the remainder of their lives and looked after their father, and someone provided better protection for the young girl than preventing the dragon or craftsman from capturing her once more.

3.3 Katie and Her Best Friend

Katie often felt isolated. She had no friends. She was okay with her parents' relocation. Nobody was left behind; therefore, she didn't feel any sadness. She was eight when they relocated. It was not significantly different from their previous residence. Outside, children were riding bicycles, playing, and climbing trees. Her mother observed her observing children playing outside. Mom instructed her to play with them. Katie left. She desired to participate but was afraid. She attempted to request a game but was unable to. She instead walked. She enjoyed the calm of the town. People were generous. She walked to the lake in town. Her face was blasted by cold air. Beautiful lake. She opted to sit there after admiring the seat. She would visit daily and possibly bring others.

She often visited the lake after school. She stated that she could spend hours there and possibly even live there. She carried food in her backpack at all times. Her stomach growled as she composed a lake-themed sonnet. She set her notebook and pen down to eat. A sound interrupted her chewing. She was astonished. In all of her days there, she had never heard anything odd. She saw no one when she looked around. She observed motion in the lake. She approached the lake inquisitively. As she approached, she seized her sandwich in her hand. It stopped close to the water. An aquatic object splashed Katie. She rubbed her eyes and observed a new sight.

Dragon: She was awestruck. When she fell, her lunch also fell. She experienced panic. Massive dragon. She was silent. The sight frightened her. The dragon buried its neck, leaving its eyes visible. Katie sensed something in the eyes of the dragon. Her eyes were lonesome. Katie stood and walked over. She handed her sandwich to the dragon. He stood still. The dragon pursued the sandwich that she dropped into the lake. Moments later, the dragon reemerged from the water. She was drenched but did not mind. She chuckled. The dragon walked up to her. She made contact with his nose. Its scales were not irritating. She met it. The dragon saluted Katie with a nod. Katie grew close to the dragon. Katie every day brought her friend five additional sandwiches. She informed the dragon of her schooling. As she sang and danced, the dragon would nod in approval. She was no longer lonely. She was even fond of the dragon. Her instructor recommended that each student prepare and recite a poem about their closest friend. Her poems were composed beside the water. She read the passage to the dragon. Dragon tapped Katie on the breast. The dragon gave its approval. So she believed. Katie read it in class next. Only in her poetry did a dragon appear. Her peers mocked her imagined dragon companion. She convinced them that the dragon was real. She vowed to confirm its authenticity.

After class, her students went to the lake. She determined that there was a dragon in the lake. The dragon evoked reverence. Some were afraid, but she quelled their fears. Her classmates went to the lake every day after school. They paid her and the dragon a visit. Everyone performed music and danced. She wished it wouldn't end. She cherished her numerous friends. No longer isolated. She went to the lake one weekend morning to see her best buddy. When she came, she noticed the dragon's head on the ground. She knelt next to it and provided comfort. She observed gloom in its eyes. The nose of the dragon rubbed its chin. Katie detected the dragon's departure. She sobbed while hugging its nose. Her best friend could not depart. The dragon then dove underwater. Katie rose. She witnessed the dragon erupt from the water and disappear into the clouds. Wept throughout the night. Her best friend was gone. The majority of her classmates did not return afterward. No dragon, no sense in going back. Some individuals desired to play at the lake.

Each day, fewer people returned until none remained. Katie started over. On the lake, she was by herself. She was unperturbed. She awaited her closest companion day after day. She would keep the return of the dragon a secret. She delivers an additional five sandwiches. Katie observed the horizon while seated beside the lake. The cold wind enveloped her. She hid her face between her knees. She gradually acknowledged her loneliness after frequent denials. Wept. Painful. The sound surprised her. She looked upward and saw no one. She was awaiting a dragon. She studied the individual seated next to her. A schoolmate. She asked, "Dylan?" She was disregarded. "Where has the dragon gone?" He silently gazed towards the horizon. She was irate. My best friend has departed. Her weeping returns. She dried her eyes and inquired, "May I depart?" Stop visiting the lake like everyone else." "I didn't come for the dragon," he stated with a smile. She questioned, "Why have you come?" He asked, "Want to be friends?" "You're my friend?" "Yes." I was too frightened to inquire sooner. I asked too late when I finally did so. Students flocked to the lake. I assumed you had sufficient friends because you had so many. Katie sat beside him and said, "Everyone wanted to be my friend because I had a dragon", "They are all fools," he declared. Katie offered him dinner, saying, "You're cool without the dragon". They were friends after that.

3.4 The Dragon's Eggs

Once there was a castle. You could discover it was an old ruin by following the twisting route behind Luca's house, across the chicken coop with its stunning chicks, up past the cobbly rocks, and through a thicket of trees. When the trees cleared, it felt like the top of the world. From there, you could see down to the green, high river. On the right stood a small town with old, brown, mossy buildings.

There was a field and a trailer park left of the river. Luca thought they were all apparitions from up here because they were far below. A raging river and honking cars in the streets below would sound like a scratch in the ear; nothing genuine. Even the bees' humming was louder than anything below. Luca could smell honey from the trail. Luca saw the Castle as a sentry guarding these unreal things. You couldn't hear anyone calling you up here, so homework didn't exist, and you didn't have to go home for lunch. Castle was impenetrable. Luca loped up to the wall of the Castle with nettle-stung legs. He tapped.

Graca smiled at him from the Castle. Luca: "You've been gone forever." Graca: "I found something." "Look!" She held out a flawless quartz crystal. Egg-shaped. It had grey lines and looked beautiful, like it was sculpted. Luca uttered a gasp of awe. "From where?" Graca was pleased. "Where?" "Back corner." I was cleaning. We could make it into a room if it rains up here. I moved those branches" Luca observed his friend's branches and leaves beside the door. Inside, where Graca spotted the egg, it was semi-covered by a roof or floor—it was so old you couldn't tell. Graca's spotless floor looked great. Sticks, rocks, and other debris were gone. The floor now resembled a real house. Ownership. Luca remained mute. Graca whispered, "The thing is-" "I lifted a big rock and found—look!" Graca led Luca to the opposite side. It was a hole a daring child could crawl through. Luca exclaimed and fell to his hands and knees to see what was on the other side. Darkness prevented much visibility. The corridor was lighted enough to see that the tunnel had extended and then turned. Graca told Luca, "I found the egg. It looked like a dragon's egg." Luca scoffed, "No dragons." Graca: "I've heard about dragon eggs. Cracking them reveals crystals." Luca was curious. He sat and thought. Why suppose there's more inside? "I found it at the tunnel's edge." Here Graca pointed to a new tunnel section. "There's another one over there." Luca hated crowded places. He detested hats, scarves, and other coverings. On rainy days, while his pals stacked beds, he played Monopoly. But a dragon's egg was too fascinating. "Should we try to get it?" he inquired, excited and afraid. Graca said, "I tried. Too big." "You're shorter. You'd fit better." When Luca heard this, his stomach quivered. He stared at Graca's egg again and begged to hold it. He didn't want one until he held it. Anything. Warm white. Its pale beauty and grey veins resembled an animal. He'd keep a dragon's egg in his pocket and touch it when he was scared. It appeared magical. He chose. He removed his coat. He said, "I'll enter." When he initially put his knees on the cold stone floor, he couldn't breathe of dread. As he went under the low stone roof, he felt it press against him as if the tunnel were made of jagged teeth, and he crept into a large chilly animal's mouth. He could only move his legs and hands forward-back, forward-back until he clutched the dragon's egg and could crawl out again. He gasped when he reached the dragon's egg, where the tunnel turned.

A bit further on, paleness sparkled. Turning his head, he noticed the dragon's eggs where the tunnel emerged. Six feet further. There was a light shining from someplace, and in the shaft, it appeared like a heap of pearls, smokey and shining, waiting for

Luca to draw them out with him. Simultaneously, he heard an inhuman shriek that was not Graca's. "Graca?" he asked weakly, unable to turn his head. He heard no reply; she must have gone outside and couldn't hear him. The sound originated from where the dragon's eggs were. A wailing sound resonated in the room and tunnels, making its origin unclear. Luca noticed an awful, terrifying fragrance that didn't come from him. It smelled unpleasant and stale. Luca knew cramped rooms often harbored bats and stagnant ponds, but this was something warm and animal, furry or clawed; possibly an animal that didn't want to share dragon's eggs with a small lad on all fours. Luca's heartbeat was a drum. He tried to reach the dragon's eggs without moving, but they stayed coldly, mockingly, out of reach. The animal howled again, and Luca realized it was the dragon. Now, he knew a dragon dwelt there. First, eggs told him. In addition to the howling, he heard clawing. Luca shivered. His forearm hair stood up. He held his egg and retreated. He didn't want to face a dragon, even if the eggs urged him to take them all and enjoy them. When the dragon cried out, Luca stopped moving backward. The lad listened, heart-pounding, skin-tingling. The second time, Luca knew he wasn't wrong. Painful dragon. He couldn't swallow. He was stuck in a broken-stone tunnel and refused to move. He couldn't leave a sorrowful animal; he heard every sadness in its scream. As though in pity, heated breath rushed into the passage. It reeked. Luca was prepared. Slowly, he crept toward the dragon. He wept. Luca rounded the corner and saw the fat, fuzzy dragon sprawled on stones. The teacher's dog, Buster. Luca saw it had

73

fallen through a ceiling hole and couldn't move. Luca crawled to Buster, who whimpered. He smelled the dog's relief in his hot breaths and stinky licks. The dog was scarier than Luca. Luca climbed out of the ceiling hole and spotted Graca digging outside the castle. Graca's mother rescued Buster.

Afterward, they returned and collected all sixteen dragon eggs, putting them on a treasure mountain in their new playhouse. Graca proposed splitting one with a stone. Inside was white, grey-seamed stone, just like the outside. Luca said, "Don't split, I prefer not knowing". The fifteen remaining dragon's eggs remained in the castle's newly cleaned corner, appreciated by all but guarding their secrets.

3.5 The Dragon Who Couldn't Puff

Once upon a time, a small dragon was the cutest you had ever seen. He was no larger than the size of your thumb. He appeared to have been fashioned from a sparkling green crystal. He possessed pearlescent scales and a purple, spiked backbone. His teeth were sharp and white. He was a beautiful specimen. Tucker was his name.

Tucker resided in an individual's pencil case. He was an assortment of house dragons. Perhaps you are unfamiliar with house dragons. Few individuals are aware of them. However, they reside in various locations and dwelling types and are quite common.

They take up residence in fruit bowls, flower vases, and the backs of toilet drawers. They are invisible throughout the day and only appear at night during the summer when the moon is three-quarters full. They prefer to spend the remainder of their time sleeping whiskery, plump, chocolatey dreams of twinkling stars, sparkling quartz, and zippy little motorcars due to their laziness and comfort.

Nonetheless, this tale occurred during one of those summers when the moon was three-quarters full, and Tucker was fully awake. The small dragon had slept well for the previous nine months and had the urge to do something enjoyable. He observed that the larger house dragons were adept at puffing fire and thought he would also like to discover how to do so.

Ferndale, the mother of Tucker, was preparing hot chocolate in a bottle cap. She blew tiny hot puffs that caused the mug to sparkle. Tucker thought it would be delightful to prepare himself a cup of hot chocolate. He curled up next to her and observed her for some time. He felt it appeared simple.

Consequently, when she flew out to munch on the pests on the basil bushes, leaving the hot mug on the windowsill, Tucker tilted forward and took a tentative puff. However, nothing occurred. Nothing at all.

He blew harder. A huge blue flame erupted from his mouth and nose. Oh no! His eyebrows burst into flames!

Tucker's older sister Mollymook tripped over her snout, laughing. She was observing the dog's dish. Tucker glowed a deep green shade. He rushed into the kitchen and hid for some time in the refrigerator, placing his face in a container of cream to cool it.

75

Eventually, a squeaking sound was heard, and his mother's beautiful blue face appeared through the fridge seal. "What are you doing here?" she questioned. "Why is your face all white?"

Tucker was embarrassed and refused to discuss it. But Mollymook had revealed all to her. "Don't worry about what your sister says", Tucker's mother instructed "do you know what occurred the first time Mollymook attempted to blast fire? She made an extremely obnoxious sound! Everyone believed it was Grandpa".

Tucker giggled. "How do you puff?" he inquired.

"Well" his mother began. "Your lips are twisted like this. And your picture singing the first note of Happy Birthday. And you simply exhale and have faith that it will occur".

Tucker tried. Nothing occurred. He stated, "I don't want to do it anyway." "Don't give up", his mother said "if you give up, you will never accomplish your goal".

Tucker scowled. He was unwilling to hear that and had chosen not to practice, and he did not. So he did not, and for the duration of that period, he was a dragon without a breath.

But one day, as the moon became fuller, Tucker checked his watch and noticed that winter was approaching. And soon, he would have to return to his long seasonal slumber with visions of ice cream and bunnies to keep, icy waves, and a chilling chill. Suddenly, Tucker realized how cold it was, where Tucker normally hibernated at the bottom of the potato dish. Suddenly, he thought it would be good to have a hot water bottle. One that he could snuggle up with, and when it became cold, he could simply puff on it to warm it up again.

Despite not being anyone's birthday, Tucker repeatedly performed his puff in the baby's nursery. He knew no one would spot him in the baby's room since all the house dragons were terrified of humans, especially giant bald ones with one large, gleaming tooth the same size as an adult house dragon! However, Tucker did not fear the infant because she was small as he was and a genuinely pleasant person.

So Tucker curled up between two teddy bears and puffed and puffed in the dark to the sound of the baby sleeping. A variety of offensive sounds emanated. Large flames and small squeaks and sparkles erupted uninhibitedly. The baby did not hear a thing.

Countless hours slipped by. Tucker's forehead was scorched, and his cheeks hurt. He ultimately realized that he could not learn to puff in a single night. He would have to practice for much longer. This year, he would not have a hot water bottle throughout the winter. He had to wait till the following year and practice much more before he could learn to puff.

However, it was fairly pleasant and warm. Even though Tucker could not puff this winter, he had discovered a cozy bed. He curled himself inside the back seam of the teddy bear and found a warm location to spend the winter. Next year, he would simply have to practice more.

Chapter 4: Stories about Princesses

4.1 The Courteous Prince

Once upon a time, a handsome Prince fell madly in love with a noble-born but lower-ranking young lady. The monarch was furious that his son was attracted to this young woman, and he resolved to separate the pair. He dispatched the court's high chancellor to an elderly witch for counsel.

After nine days of deliberation, the old woman murmured the following response: "I shall woo the young lady until civility triumphs." The king stated, "I'm not entirely sure whatever the old hag means. However, if she will remove this girl from the Prince's sight, I can organize his marriage to a person of his status". The young lady vanished after a few days, and the Prince could locate no trace of her. He vowed that if he could not wed his one true love, he would remain single for the remainder of his life.

On a sunny day at the end of October, the young Prince and some nobles went hunting. The hounds were chasing a stunning deer so crafty and swift, that the nobility gradually lost view of the target and abandoned the pursuit. The young Prince, a renowned horseman, resumed the hunt. He rode for many miles across the rolling hills until eventually, in a wooded ravine, the exhausted deer was cornered by the hounds and slain by the Prince.

The royal hunter didn't realize how shadowy the ravine was and how menacing the evening sky looked until after he had obtained the treasure. He was certain that he had traveled too far from the palace to turn back and had no idea where he was. He threw the prey onto the back of his horse, whistled for his dogs, and then rode cautiously down the wooded valley, thinking about where he would spend the night. "There's not much sign of hospitality in this barren region," he thought to himself. "Maybe I could make the best of it and find a safe spot in one of the rocky hollows" as darkness grew, he continued to ride. A curve in the valley led him to a patch of moorland, and he spotted the dark silhouette of an abandoned hunting hall a short distance away. "A dreary-looking inn", pondered the Prince "one will have to play both host and visitor in this location. Yet, I am accompanied by my faithful canines and loyal steed, and the prey will supply a scrumptious meal for all of us". He got off his horse and walked towards the ancient ruin.

He forced open the door with minimal effort. The rattling of its old hinges produced peculiar echoes around the corridor. The Prince took his horse into one of the little chambers before proceeding with his hounds to the enormous dining hall, where he started a fire in the massive hearth and roasted some deer for supper. As he waited for the meat to cook, he observed the increasingly powerful wind, which made a noise around the deserted ruins and rattled the doors and windows without interruption. In the room next door, the horse was stamping the ground uneasily and every few moments, the hounds would raise their heads up to the sky and howl in a strange way.

The Prince pondered before the fire, "This is All Hallow's Eve, the night that witches and ghosts celebrate. However, I'd rather be in this empty hall than on the storm-ravaged moor", he removed the meat from the fire and prepared to have supper. A sudden gust of wind blew open a massive door towards the far end of the hallway, and a tall, ghostly woman entered the chamber. Her lean form was dressed in drab clothing that flowed for yards on the ground. Long, gray hair cascaded freely down her back. The Prince could discern her lifeless eyes and skeletal features by the fire's flickering light. He was a courageous guy, yet this spectral being filled him with terror and despair.

The hounds laid aside their deer bones and crept closer to their master, who was rendered mute. The gray phantom advanced slowly down the hallway towards the Prince, extending a hard, bony finger at him and inquiring in a hollow tone, "Are you a polite knight?", the Prince answered with a trembling voice "I will do as you ask. What do you need?"; "Go to the moorlands and collect enough heather to make a bed for me in the turret chamber", the ghostly figure murmured. It was a strange quest, but the Prince was glad to be able to find an excuse to get away from her. He jumped up and raced out into the raging night in search of heather. He collected as much as he could pack into his tartan and then came back to the manor, where the unearthly guest was waiting. She showed him the direction to the tower chamber by going down the chamber and climbing up a partially destroyed staircase. Here, he made her a bed of heather and wrapped it with his plaid. At its conclusion, she indicated the exit and dismissed him. "Sleep well", remarked the Prince with courtesy.

Then, chilly and exhausted, he went to the hall and fell asleep in front of the fading flames. When he awoke, the windows were illuminated by the sun. The Prince wasted little time preparing to leave as he vividly recalled the ghostly apparition from the previous evening. "Without a doubt, she left before the rooster crowed," he claimed. I doubted if she had left my beloved plaid in the room at the top of the tower. The cold autumn air was sharp and biting. I will go take a look. He quickly ran up the broken stairs.

When he reached the top, to his surprise, the chamber's door opened, and his lost sweetheart appeared. "How did you get here?" exclaimed the Prince. "Where is the ghostly figure?" She stated, "Last night, I was the grey ghost and tonight, thou wilt change thy shape once more?" he inquired in shock. "Never again", stated the young woman "to separate us, a wicked witch cast a spell over me, transforming me into the horrifying form you saw last night. However, you have broken her evil spell". The Prince, whose face was glowing with joy, asked "Tell me how". "The witch's spell could not be undone until a knight served me, despite my hideous appearance. Through thy kindness, thou hast broken the enchantment", the maiden said. When the king heard of his son's encounter in the hunting hall, he exclaimed, "Now I understand what the old witch indicated by her prophecy".

4.2 The Bird with Nine Heads

Once upon a time, a queen and a king gave birth to a daughter. One day, while the daughter was playing in the garden, a fierce tempest suddenly appeared and carried her away. This storm was created by the nine-headed bird, who had abducted the princess and taken her to its lair. The ruler had no idea where his daughter had gone, so he proclaimed in the kingdom: "Whoever brings back the princess shall wed her!"A young man took the Princess to his cave when he spotted the nine-headed bird. This cave, however, was amidst a vertical rock face. It could not be climbed up from underneath, nor could it be climbed down from above. As the young man walked around the rock, another youngster approached him and inquired why he was there.

Therefore, the first youth informed the other young man that the king's daughter was in his cave. This male visitor was aware of his obligations. He gathered his companions. Once he entered the cavern, he witnessed the princess of the king seated there, treating the injury of the nine-headed creature, whose tenth head had been chomped by the divine dog and was still bleeding. However, the Princess signaled to the boy to hide, and he did so. After the princess tended to the bird's wound, the nine-headed creature felt so calm that all of its nine heads went to sleep.

The young man came out of his hiding place and cut off his nine heads with a knife. But the princess of the king said, "It would be better if I go first, and then you come after me." "No," the boy replied "I'll stay here until you are safe." Initially, the king's daughter was unwilling, but she eventually gave in to persuasion and jumped into the basket. She removed a long hairpin from her hair, split it in half, and handed the boy one half while keeping the other.

She also gave him her silk scarf and told him to look after both of her presents. Nevertheless, when the other man saved the princess of the king, he took her away with him and abandoned the young man in the cave, despite his desperate appeals. The visitor then walked around the cave. There, he observed many maidens who had been abducted by the nine-head bird and had died of starvation. In addition, a fish was affixed to the wall with four nails.

When he had the fish in his grasp, it changed into a beautiful young man that expressed his gratitude for being saved, and they decided to become brothers. Soon after, the first youth began to feel hungry.He stepped out of the cave and searched for something to eat, only to find rocks. Suddenly, he noticed an enormous dragon that was licking a stone. The boy copied the dragon's behavior and soon his hunger disappeared.

The first young person inquired of the dragon how they could get out of the cave, and the dragon gestured in the direction of its tail, as if implying that they could ride on it. So, he ascended and instantly he was back on the ground and the dragon had disappeared. He kept going until he found a tortoiseshell full of stunning pearls. However, these were magical pearls; if thrown into the fire, they would not burn, and if thrown into the water, they would break up and you could walk across them.

The teenager removed the pearls from the tortoiseshell and placed them in his pocket. Not soon after he approached the shore, he began to swim. He threw a gem into the ocean, and the sea immediately parted, revealing the seadragon. Who is troubling me in my realm? shouted the sea dragon. The youth responded, "I discovered pearls in a tortoiseshell, threw one into the sea, and now the waters have separated for me. Come into the sea with me, and we will dwell there together", replied the dragon if this were true. Then, the boy identified him as the same dragon he had encountered in the cave.

The elderly dragon declared that the young man had become like a son to him, since he had saved his son and formed a bond of brotherhood with him. He welcomed him with warmth and hospitality, offering him food and drink. His friend told him one day, "My father is likely to offer you payment. Don't accept money or jewelry from him, only the small gourd flask over there."He told the old dragon that he wanted the ability to create whatever he wished. And, sure enough, the dragon informed him what he desired as a reward, to which the boy answered "Not money or jewels. All I wanted was the little gourd flask that was sitting there." the dragon was hesitant to give it up at first, however he eventually gave in.

The youth departed the dragon's fortress. When he stepped back onto dry land, he felt ravenous. A table laden with a delicious and copious dinner appeared before him. He consumed food and drink. After continuing for some time, he felt exhausted.

There, waiting for him, was an ass, which he rode. After riding, he felt that the ass's pace was too irregular, so he climbed into an approaching wagon. But the wagon jolted him too violently, and he thought, "If only I had a litter, I'd be better off". Just as he was thinking this, the litter arrived, and he sat in it. The carriers brought him to the city where the king, queen, and their daughter resided. The wedding was scheduled as soon as the other young man returned with the king's daughter.

However, the princess refused, saying: "He is not the right man. The one who saves me will come with half of the long hairpin for my hair and half of my silk handkerchief as a keepsake."The king became increasingly frustrated, proclaiming "The wedding shall occur tomorrow!" as the boy didn't arrive for a considerable amount of time, and the other youth pressured him. Subsequently, the king's daughter sadly strolled through the city's streets, exploring every crevice in search of her savior.

On the day the litter arrived, the princess noticed the young man holding half of her silk kerchief and was overjoyed, taking him to meet the king.He was asked to show his half of the lengthy pin, which fit perfectly with the other half, and the king was assured that he was the rightful and genuine savior. They experienced joy and serenity for the remainder of their lives after the deceitful groom was reprimanded and the ceremony was held.

4.3 The Princess of Canterbury

Formerly, in the county of Cumberland, there lived a nobleman with three sons, two of whom were handsome and intelligent young men, and the third a natural fool named Jack, who was frequently busy with the sheep. He wore a multicolored coat and a tassel cap, which befitted his situation.

Now, the King of Canterbury had a lovely daughter who was known for her tremendous intelligence and wit, and he issued a proclamation stating that whoever answered three questions posed by the princess would marry her and become heir to the throne upon his death. Shortly after this proclamation was released, word of it entered the ears of the nobleman's sons. The two intelligent ones decided to have a trial, but they could not dissuade their moron brother from joining them.

They could not get rid of Jack and were forced to allow him to follow them. Before long, Jack yelled with laughter and exclaimed, "I've found an egg! Put it in your pocket", the brothers instructed. A short time later, he erupted in laughter upon discovering a curved hazel stick, which he also placed in his pocket, and a third time he laughed uncontrollably upon discovering a nut. It was likewise placed alongside his other valuables.

When they reached the palace and mentioned the nature of their mission, they were promptly accepted and led to a room where the Princess and her entourage were seated. Jack, who seldom stood on ceremony, exclaimed, "What a group of beautiful women we have!" "Yes," replied the Princess, "we are beautiful women because we hold fire in our hearts." "Then cook me an egg," replied Jack, removing an egg from his pocket. "How will you get it back out?" the Princess asked. "By using a crooked stick," Jack responded, producing the hazel. "From where did that come?" questioned the Princess. "From a nut," replied Jack as he extracted the nut from his pocket. "Now that I've answered the three questions, the lady is mine." "No, no," the monarch replied."slow down. You still have the experience to endure. You must come here in one week and spend the entire night with my daughter, the Princess. If you can stay awake all night, you will marry her the next day". "But what if I can't?" Jack asked. The king responded, "Then your head shall be severed. However, you need not attempt if you choose not to". Jack returned home for a week to consider whether he should attempt to win the Princess.

Finally, he made a decision. "Well", answered Jack, "I'll give my vorton a go, so now against the king's daughter or a shepherd without a head!" He made his way to the court with his drink and bag. To reach his destination, he had to cross a river. After removing his stockings and shoes, he noticed numerous beautiful fish swimming against his feet, so he caught and placed them in his pocket. When he arrived at the palace, he knocked loudly on the entrance with his crook, and after declaring the purpose of his visit, he was instantly led to the hall where the king's daughter was waiting to see her suitors. He was seated in a plush chair, and great wines, spices, and delectable foods were brought before him. Jack, used to such stuff, ate and drank copiously, nearly falling asleep before midnight. Oh, shepherd, the lady exclaimed, "I caught you napping!" "No, my friend, I was busy fishing." "No, shepherd, there is no fishpond in the hall," the Princess exclaimed with the greatest surprise. "Regardless, I've been fishing in my pocket and have just caught a fish." "Oh my God!" she said. "Let me see it." The shepherd sneakily removed the fish from his pocket and pretended to have caught it before showing it to her. She declared it to be the nicest fish she had ever seen. Approximately half an hour later, she asked the shepherd, "Shepherd, do you believe you could get me another?" He said, "Perhaps, once I've baited my hook," and after a short time, he dragged up another fish that was even more beautiful than the first. The Princess was so pleased that she permitted him to sleep and vowed to excuse him to her father. In the morning, the Princess informed the king, much to his shock, that Jack should not be beheaded since he had been catching fish in the hall all night.

When the king heard that Jack had caught such a lovely fish in his pocket, he asked Jack to catch another in his pocket. Jack eagerly accepted the assignment, and after telling the king to lie down, he acted to fish in his pocket while concealing another fish in his hand. He then pricked the monarch with a needle, lifted the fish, and presented it to the king. His Majesty did not particularly enjoy the procedure, but he consented to the marvel of it. The Princess and Jack were wed on the same day and lived happily and prosperously for many years.

4.4 The Swineherd

Once upon a time, there was a Prince who possessed a kingdom. His domain was little, yet he desired to wed, and his name was well-known that a hundred Princesses would have replied "Yes!" and "Thank you". A rose tree grew where the Prince's father was buried; it was a beautiful rose tree that blossomed once every five years and produced only one rose. It smelt so lovely that he forgot all his problems. The Prince also owned a nightingale that sang so sweetly that it seemed like all songs resided in her throat. Thus, the rose and nightingale, his precious treasures, were given in silver caskets as gifts to a beautiful Princess, an Emperor's daughter.

When the Princess saw the gift-filled caskets, she clapped her hands in delight. She said, "If only it were a kitten!" as a rose tree with a beautiful rose emerged. The court woman said, "How lovely!" The Emperor remarked, "It's charming!" The Princess nearly shed a tear when touching it. "Fie, papa! Nothing. It is mundane and natural!", "Let's examine what's in the second coffin before we go insane" said the Emperor. So exquisite was the nightingale's singing that no one could condemn her. "Superb!

Elegant!" said the women, whose French was inferior to their neighbors. "The bird reminds me of the Empress's musical box," said the old knight. "Yes!" "Same tones, the same execution", the Emperor wept like a child as he recalled the past. The Princess prayed that it was not an actual bird.

The bearers responded, "Yes, it's authentic". Princess: "Allow the bird to fly away". Again, it's free and natural. She turned down the Prince. He applied dirt to his face, placed his cap over his ears, and knocked. Salutations, Emperor! "Am I permitted to work at the palace?" The Emperor's response was "Yes." She said, "Take care of our many pigs." The Prince attained the title "Imperial Swineherd". He toiled all day in a filthy chamber adjacent to the hovel. By sundown, he had fashioned a cooking pot. While the stew was cooking, the bells played the familiar tune "Ah, Augustine, my darling!" All gone! Unlike the rose, whoever put his finger in the kitchen-pot smoke could smell all the dishes cooking on every hearth in the city. The Princess stopped and smiled when she heard the tune; she could play "Dear Augustine" with one finger. Princess: "My slice is here. That pig farmer was cunning!" Inquire about the instrument's price.

Therefore, one of the court women ran in while wearing slippers. The woman said, "What's in the cooking pot?" The pig farmer requested ten Princess kisses. Yes, she responded. The pig farmer responded, "I cannot sell it for less", the Princess whispered, "He's impudent!" yet as she moved, the bells rang so sweetly. All is lost, Augustine! Princess stated, "Remain." Request that he receive ten kisses from my court ladies. The pig farmer responded, "No thanks". "Ten Princess kisses, or the pot is mine". Princess: "Indeed not!", "Stand in front of me so no one can see us." The court ladies stood before her and laid out their robes; the swineherd received ten kisses, while the Princess received a cooking pot. Wonderful! The pot is cooked day and night.

The court ladies were aware of what was cooking in every kitchen in the city, from the chamberlain to the cobbler. Who is eating soup, pancakes, cutlets, and eggs tonight? Wow! "Yes, but keep my identity a secret; I am the daughter of the Emperor." No one knew the Prince was anything other than a swineherd; therefore, he never went a day without working on something. When swung, he developed a rattle that played all the waltzes and jigs heard from the beginning of time. The Princess said, "That's magnificent! I've never heard anything more beautiful! Ask him how much the instrument costs, but refrain from kissing him", "She'll give him a hundred kisses," stated the woman who posed the question. The Princess shouted, "I think he's insane!" before stopping after a short distance, she stated "I am the Emperor's daughter". Yesterday, informing him that he may take the remaining court ladies. No, they replied. The Princess inquired, "What are you muttering?" You may kiss him if I may do so. I am owed everything. Thus, they returned to him. "One hundred kisses from the Princess or your own!" as she kissed, all the women surrounded her and stood still. After stepping onto the balcony, the Emperor massaged his eyes and put on his glasses. "They are ladies of the palace; I must go see!" he lifted the heels of his slippers since he had stepped on them.

Once he entered the courtyard, he proceeded stealthily, and the ladies were too preoccupied with counting kisses to see him. On the tips of his toes, he stood. As the swineherd gave the Princess her eighty-sixth kiss, he boxed the Princess' ears with his slipper upon observing what was occurring. The Emperor was enraged and ordered the Princess and the pig herder to leave the city. Princess grieved, the swineherd reprimanded, and it began to rain. "Alas! Awful Princess! I wish I had married the handsome young prince." The swineherd retreated behind a tree, washed the grime from his face, discarded his filthy attire, and emerged wearing royal robes.

The Princess was unable to resist bowing to him. "There is no noble Prince for you!" You did not cherish the rose or the nightingale, but you were eager to kiss the hovel for a trumpery toy! "You are being served." He returned to his domain and shut the door in her face before entering. Now she may sing, "Ah, Augustine! All gone!"

4.5 The White Duck

A very beautiful Princess was married to a mighty Prince, Before he could embark on a long trip and entrust his devoted wife to strangers, he had no time to look at her, talk to her, or hear her pleasant words. The Prince consoled the Princess by instructing her not to leave her high tower to avoid nasty people, foul-mouthed individuals, and unusual women. Princess swore this oath. After the Prince left, she returned to her room. She sat there without end. She eventually sat sobbing by the window until a woman went by. She was plain and caring, so she put her arms on her cane, held her chin in her palms, and spoke softly and soothingly to the Princess. "Dear little Princess, why are you so worried? Come down from your tower, gaze upon God's marvelous creation, or enter your garden to wash away your grief!" The Princess ignored the woman's fears and did not even examine them before saying, "Entering the garden is not risky; however, crossing the creek is a different matter", she didn't realize that the woman was a witch intending to destroy her joy, as she despised her contentment.

The Princess followed her into the garden and heard her plead. The garden was fed by streams coming from the mountain. The woman remarked, "The day is hot, the sun is blazing with all its might, but this wonderful little brook is so refreshing, so calming, and listen to it gurgle; why shouldn't we swim here?" "No!" She inquired, "Yet why not? Bathing cannot be dangerous!" She took off her sarafan and dove into the water when the witch smacked her on the back and told her to "swim like a white duck!" The witch donned a disguise as the Princess, bound and painted herself, and awaited the Prince in the tower. When the doorbell rang and the dog barked, she went to him and tenderly petted him. The Prince was the first person to embrace the Princess, but it was a witch. The unfortunate duck living in the sparkling stream laid eggs and had babies; two of them were healthy, but the third one was stillborn. Eventually, her children became strong and brave. She took children up, and as they descended the stream, they caught goldfish, gathered rags to make coats, ran up the banks, and surveyed the meadows. "Oh!" said the mother "No, kids. She destroyed me; she will destroy you!" refers to a witch.

The children disobeyed their mother and played in the grass before chasing ants in the courtyard of the Prince. The witch instinctively recognized them, clenched her teeth in wrath, disguised herself as a lovely woman, summoned the children to the outhouse, fed and drank them, and then put them to sleep. She commanded her attendants to ignite a blaze in the courtyard, set a kettle above it, and hone their cutlery. The two boys fell asleep, but the third brother, whom their mother asked them to carry in their bosoms so he wouldn't get cold, did not sleep and instead listened and observed. The witch enquired during the night, "Children, are you asleep?" The stillborn one replied on behalf of his siblings, "We don't dream in dreams, but we think in our minds that you aim to kill us all!" "The flames of maple logs are roaring, the cauldrons are bubbling, and the edges of the blades are being sharpened." Children, are you asleep? The stillborn's cries echoed from under his pillow, rather than those of his siblings: "We do not rest in our dreams, but our minds conceive that you wish to separate us all; the piles of maple wood are burning, the cauldrons are steaming, and the metal knives are being honed." Why was the sound the same all the time? The witch was curious. She softly stepped into the room and observed both of the brothers slumbering. She took their lives.

The white duck awoke and screamed out for her young, but they were unresponsive. She anticipated the worst. She flew trembling to the Prince's courtyard. The brothers in the Prince's courtyard were as pale as handkerchiefs and as chilly as fish fillets. She descended, landed on them, fluttered her wings around them, and exclaimed, "Kra, kra, my sweethearts!" Kra-kra, doves! I raised you in agony and fear and fed you with sorrow and tears; the dark evenings prevented me from sleeping, and no food tasted good because of you. The Prince heard the anguish, contacted his wife, and asked, "Have you heard about this unheard-of event?" "Impossible!" "Hi! Please remove this duck from the yard, servants." She circled her young and shouted, "Kra, kra, my dear lovelies! Kra-kra, doves! Your poison is the ancient, old witch; she snatched your father, my husband, and flung us into the river. She made us into white ducks while profiting as though evil were advantageous." When Prince realized a problem, he screamed, "Bring me that white duck!" The white duck circled in the air, escaping them as everyone raced to comply. When the Prince climbed onto the roof, she leaped into his hands and fell to her knees.

The Prince grabbed her by the arm and tearfully exclaimed, "Behind me is a white birch tree, and before me is an attractive young lady!" She instructed her kids how to secure a small pouch of alive and verbal water from a magpie's home, sprinkled the living water on them, made them tremble, and afterward splashed them with the verbal water, which prompted them to start talking and conversing. In an instant, the Prince saw his family safe and sound. They chose to be content with each other and opted to do what was right rather than wrong. Under the Prince's direction, the witch was tethered to the horse's tail and dragged over the steppe. The air birds devoured her flesh, and the ferocious winds dispersed her bones, leaving no trace or monument.

4.6 Briar Rose

O nce, a queen and king controlled a distant realm with the aid of fairies. This royal couple had abundant money, wonderful food and drink, beautiful clothes, and a daily coach trip, but they had no children, which greatly pained them. The Queen was strolling alongside the river at the base of the garden when she spotted a fish that had dragged itself out of the water and was lying on the shoreline, practically lifeless.

The queen felt empathy towards the tiny fish and put it back into the river. Before it swam away, it lifted its head out of the water and expressed its thanks. "I am aware of your wish, and it will be fulfilled. You will soon have a daughter". The prophecy of the small fish came true, and the queen gave birth to a beautiful baby girl. The king was mesmerized by her beauty and vowed to host a grand celebration to introduce her to the entire country. He requested help from his relatives, aristocrats, companions, and people from the local area. The queen answered, "I'll also invite some fairies, so they'll be beneficial to our daughter". There were thirteen fairies in the kingdom, but the king and queen had only twelve golden plates, so they gave one away with no request. Following the banquet, the fairies gathered in a circle and presented the young Princess with their finest presents.

One gave her goodness; another gave her wealth; another gave her beauty, and so on until she received everything well. Just as eleven completed her benediction, a loud sound echoed throughout the courtyard, signaling the arrival of the mysterious thirteenth fairy. She was adorned with a black cap, a broomstick in her hand, and a set of dark wings and shoes.. As she was not invited to the banquet, she became enraged, reprimanded the king and queen, and plotted her revenge. Therefore, she stated "At the age of fifteen, the king's daughter will be slain by a spindle". The twelfth of the good fairies, who had not yet given her a present, approached her and informed her that the evil desire must be granted but that she could mitigate its ill effects.

Therefore, her gift was that the king's daughter, when wounded by the spindle, would not die but slumber for a hundred years. The monarch sought to protect his child from evil by purchasing and destroying every spindle. Everyone who knew the Princess adored her because she was beautiful, kind, sage, and well-mannered.

The king and queen were abroad on her fifteenth birthday, leaving her alone in the palace. So she traveled alone, observing all the halls and apartments until she reached an old tower with a narrow staircase and a door. The door opened when she turned the golden key to reveal an older woman engaged in spinning. What are you doing, motherly figure? The older woman hummed and nodded as the wheel buzzed. The Princess picked up the spindle and started to spin it. The spindle pierced her and she collapsed lifelessly onto the floor, as the fairy had foretold. She wasn't actually dead, but had instead fallen into a deep slumber. The king and queen, who had just returned home, and all of their court also fell asleep. As everyone lay down to sleep, even the fire on the hearth went out; the kitchen boy, who was being pulled by his chef by his hair, let go and both fell asleep, and the butler, who was secretly sipping some ale from a jug, eventually dozed off with it still at his lips; thus everything stayed still and slumbered peacefully. A large hedge of thorns grew around the palace, and each year it grew taller and denser until not even the roof or chimneys of the ancient castle could be seen. As the king's daughter was known throughout the land, the beautiful sleeping Briar Rose prompted the sons of various monarchs to attempt to break into the palace. None of them could, as thorns and bushes seized them like hands, and they perished in misery.

Years later, a king's son arrived in that territory. An older man told him that behind the thorny thicket was a beautiful palace where a beautiful Princess named Briar Rose slept with her court. He described how his grandfather informed him that other Princes who attempted to burst through the underbrush perished. The Prince said, "This will not frighten me; I will see the Briar Rose". The older man tried to stop him, but he continued. This day marked the end of a century, and when the Prince neared the thicket, he saw nothing but lovely flowering plants, which he navigated with ease.

They advanced at him as densely as ever. Then he arrived at the palace, where he observed sleeping dogs in the court, horses in the stables, and pigeons with their heads tucked beneath their wings on the roof. When he stepped into the palace, he saw the flies taking a break on the walls, the saliva was motionless, the butler had a mug of beer close to his mouth, the servant had a bird perched on her lap, and it seemed as though the chef was preparing to hit the young one with a spoon. He arrived at the old tower and stepped inside Briar Rose's chamber. His footsteps were muffled and all he could hear was his own breathing, which was loud in the silence. He saw her lying peacefully on the sofa beside the window and couldn't help but marvel at her beauty. He leaned in to give her a kiss.

As soon as he kissed her, she awoke, smiled, and the couple left together. The king, queen, and court soon awoke and gazed in astonishment at one another. Briar Rose and the Prince were wed and lived happily ever after

4.7 The Elfin Knight

Around the towers of a grey stone castle, a harsh and loud autumn wind blew. Janet, one of the most beautiful Scotch maidens, was listening to an old nurse regale her with tales of Elfland in the bower of my lady. The hallways resonated with Janet's happy laugh when the narrative ended. The elderly nurse nodded her head fervently and stated, "It is widely known, my lassie, that the inhabitants of Elfland enjoy the Scottish highlands and hollows. Come closer, and I'll share a secret with you." Janet leaned forward as the old woman murmured, "An Elfin Knight by the name of Tam Lin stalks the moorland bordering your father's farm". No damsel dares approach the enchanted location because if she were to fall under the enchantment of this Elfin Knight, she would be compelled to pay him a valuable gem as ransom. Janet chuckled as she said, "One glance of the Elfin Knight would be like the rarest stone I possess. I hope that I can see him!", "Quiet!" exclaimed her terrified nurse. "Nay, nay, my lady!" Mortals must have no contact with the inhabitants of Elfland. Tomorrow is Halloween, the night when fairies travel abroad, so steer clear of the moorlands at this time of year. The following morning, however, Janet wrapped her golden braids around her

101

head, donned her green kirtle, and hopped gently to the enchanted moor. As she approached, she saw beautiful flowers blooming as if it were midsummer. She knelt to gather some roses when she suddenly heard the softest silvery music. She looked around and saw the most handsome knight she had ever seen riding toward her. His milk-white horse, which moved faster than the breeze, was shod with silver shoes, and small silver bells hung from the bridle. When the knight approached, he dismounted his horse and asked, "Fair Janet, why do you pick roses in Elfland?" The maiden's heart was racing, and the flowers fell from her hands, but she responded with pride, "I've come to visit Tam Lin, the Elfin Knight." "He stands before you," the knight declared. "Have you come to Elfland to rescue him?" At these remarks, Janet's bravery faltered because she feared that he would cast a spell upon her. When the knight noticed that she was trembling, he added, "Have no fear, Lady Janet; you shall hear my tale. I was born to noble parents. When I was nine years old, I once started hunting with my dad. Now, by coincidence, we became isolated from one another, and misfortune befell me. The stumble of my good horse knocked me to the ground, where I lay dazed. There, the Fairy Queen discovered me and transported me to that green hill. And while living in Fairyland is delightful, I desire to be among mortals once more." Janet responded, "Then why don't you ride away to your home?", "Alas, I cannot accomplish it unless a valiant woman is willing to assist me." In three ways, she must demonstrate her bravery. She must first be willing to meet me here on the enchanting moors. That you have done, the knight stated. Then, he

102

stopped and pleaded with Janet's eyes. Her fear faded, and she inquired, "In what other methods must a young woman demonstrate courage?", "She must overcome her dread of him". "You have also done this," said the knight. "Tell me the third method, Tam Lin, for I think I am the servant who will release you." Janet, only my real love, can demonstrate her courage on the third path. The maiden then responded, "I am your genuine love, Tam Lin." "Then take my advice, courageous lady. This evening is Halloween. The Fairy Queen and all of her knights will ride forth at midnight. If you dare to win your true love, you must wait until the Fairy Queen and her Elfin Knights come through Milescross. I shall follow in her wake." "How will I recognize you amid so many knights, Tam Lin?" Lady Janet inquired. "I will bike in the third group of trailing individuals. Let the Fairy Queen's first and second troops pass and search for me in the third." This final group will consist of only three knights; one will ride a black horse, one will ride a brown horse, and the third will ride a milk-white horse, stated the knight, referring to his mount. "My right hand would be gloved, Janet, but my left hand will be exposed," he added. By these signals, you'll recognize me." "I will know you without fail," Janet affirmed. "Wait calmly until I am close, then leap forward and grab me. When the fairies discover you carrying me, they will transform me into a variety of forms. Fear not, but secure me in your arms. I will finally assume my human form. If you have the fortitude to do so, you will liberate your real love from the fairies' control." Janet declared, "I have sufficient bravery to accomplish all you ask." They confirmed this agreement with a

103

kiss before parting ways. The night was dark, and the path to Milescross was frightening. However, Janet threw her green cloak over her shoulders and dashed to the enchanted moor. On the entire journey, she repeated to herself, "On Halloween at midnight, I will rescue my real love, Tam Lin, from Elfland." She hid in Milescross and waited. How the sea breeze howled across the moorland! Suddenly, she heard the joyous tinkling of distant music, and she saw a glimmering light moving forward in the distance. Janet could feel her heartbeat, yet she continued to stand unafraid. The Fairy Queen and her court were on the go. The beautiful queen rode at the head of her 1st merry company of knights and ladies of honor, her jeweled girdle and crown gleaming in the darkness. The second group rapidly passed, and now the third set of three knights had arrived. One rode a black horse, another a brown horse, and the milk-white steed arrived last. Janet could see that one of the rider's hands was gloved while the other was not. Then, the girl leaped to her feet. She quickly grasped the reins of the milk-white horse, dismounted the rider, and wrapped her green shawl around him. The Elfin Knights were agitated, and the Fairy Queen yelled, "Tam Lin! Tam Lin!" Someone has captured Tam Lin, the most jovial knight in my company!" Then the most bizarre events transpired. Rather than Tam Lin, Janet was holding a bearded lion that was desperately trying to escape. However, she recalled the knight's warning. "Hold me fast, and do not fear me." The following instant, she grasped a fire-breathing dragon, which nearly slipped from her hold, but she strengthened her grip and recalled Tam Lin's words. The dragon

104

transformed into a flaming shrub, and flames sprung out in all directions, but Janet was unharmed. Then, she clutched in her arms a flowering tree with branching branches. Finally, Tam Lin, her real love, appeared. When the Fairy Queen realized that none of her spells could terrify Janet, she said angrily, "The maiden has won a noble groom who was my bravest warrior!" "Alas! Tam Lin has vanished into Elfland". The fairy train continued into the darkness. Lady Janet and Tam Lin hurriedly returned to the stone castle. Tam Lin, who was a Scottish Earl, and Lady Janet, the most courageous woman in Scotland, were wedded there shortly after a bridal banquet was prepared.

Chapter 5: Stories about Adventures

5.1 The Knight and the Griffin

Annually, Frank's family traveled to San Francisco. They went to Rupert and Elaine's residence.

Before Frank was born, his family engaged in this activity. He was unconcerned. Rupert and Elaine were his two favorite individuals. He had fun. After his initial visit, he could not wait to return. His parents also appreciated it. When they arrived, Rupert was rocking on the front porch. Frank went towards Mr. Rupert. At the front porch, he halted. Then, he hugged Rupert. Inside, he hugged Elaine. She pets his head gently. Frank always expected this from her. He admired her for her gentleness. He disclosed to Elaine his age as ten. Frank's parents greeted Elaine. He left to join Rupert. Rupert's tales inspired him to travel. The stories of Rupert intrigued him. There was something extraordinary about hearing Rupert's tales. Frank strolled outdoors to join Rupert, who was appreciating the view.

"Are you prepared, son?" He grinned and happily nodded his head. "Take a seat," he suggested. Frank grabbed Rupert's stool. Rupert leaned forward to listen to Frank's narrative. Frank awaited Rupert's introduction with patience. He was overflowing with enthusiasm. Rupert took a breath and began. Once, a knight lived. Among Magon's most dangerous warriors. He and his fellow knights won countless wars. In their kingdom, peace prevailed for a very long time. One day, the peace was threatened.

The populace became restless when a griffin assaulted one of the kingdom's villages. The king ordered his knights to slaughter every griffin in the kingdom so that his subjects may once again feel secure. The knight sought the griffin as directed by his lord. The knight believed that killing the griffin would enhance his family's reputation. He went mountaineering. A sage older man had told him that griffins are concealed in the mountains' depths. He traveled nonstop. He slept outside. He shivered at the wind's chill. He heard peculiar forest sounds. His sword grip strengthened. He stopped in a town. Before he set out on his quest, he was fed and lodged. He inquired of a villager whether a griffin had previously frightened them. The villager replied negatively, and their society was always peaceful. However, the mountain made odd noises. Nobody ventured to ascend the mountain since no one knew what it was. They were afraid of monsters. After listening to the villager's remarks, the knight wished to climb the mountain. He consumed food and slept all night. The following morning, he expressed his gratitude and left the community. To locate the griffin, he climbed the mountain. Elaine delivered juice and cookies to Frank and coffee to Rupert. Elaine abandoned the tray and walked inside. Frank devoured one of Elaine's cookies and hoped he could consume them indefinitely. Rupert sipped some coffee before continuing his story. The knight scaled a mountain. He navigated the forest with care. He heard all of it. He grasped the handle of his sword in preparation for unsheathing it. A cave prevented him from reaching the mountain's peak. He approached with caution. He detected sounds. He unsheathed his sword and loosened up. The griffin must be found within. True.

The griffin rushed at him. The griffin evaded his blade. The griffin was the taller animal. It was standing with its wings out. It ripped at his armor with its sharp claws. The greatest smith crafted his armor in the kingdom. Strong griffin. With his armor, he evaded its claws, but the blow nearly killed him. He withdrew. Heavy respiration. He prepared for another swing. The griffin charged once more. Then he brandished his sword. As the griffin approached, he swung his sword ferociously. The griffin avoided the knight, but its arm was severed. Its arm had been severed. The griffin collided with the cave's wall. Thus, the knight was capable of killing the beast. He charged the griffin while preparing to strike with his sword. Then, he felt a rumbling emanating from the cave. He halted abruptly. He glanced toward the sounds and regained his equilibrium. Another possible griffin. His astonishment was caused by younglings hiding beneath a rock. Young griffins exhibited apprehension.

The younglings swarmed the griffin. The griffin's wing shielded the youngling. He spotted a griffin. It was worn out and in pain. He recognized that the griffin was protecting its young. No monster, just a mom is guarding her kids. He sheathed his weapon and departed. The following day, he returned to the cave with three wild boars and some medicine. The injured griffin continued to reside within the cave. His sword and armor dropped. He attempted to comfort the griffin. He fed the young boars of the griffin. His remedy cured the griffin's wounds. After recovering, the griffin left the cave. He did not care that he returned to the king's castle empty-handed. He gave up his knighthood. The monarch bid farewell. "The knight and his bride lived happily together." On a mountain, they made their home. While viewing the horizon, he spotted a winged creature. It approached and landed alongside their residence. Griffin and juvenile. Since he had last seen them, their offspring had grown. The griffin mysteriously discovered him. Perhaps it looked for him all day. The griffin was appreciated. His wife was stunned. He carried his sword into the wild. He came back with four wild boars. They were joined by the griffin and its young for lunch.

The griffin and its offspring began paying an annual visit to the knight and his wife. The knight waited for his companion's return. Rupert declared, "End" Frank applauded Rupert's conclusion while grinning. Rupert's finest tale. Frank and his family bid their goodbyes and departed. Frank asked his father why they were required to visit Elaine and Rupert annually on the way home. He never inquired as to why his father enjoyed visiting so much. His father said with a grin, "Rupert was a buddy of your grandfather." Your grandfather promised to visit it just once a year. And I'll keep it. "I hope you retain your dedication." "Sure." Never tire of Rupert and Elaine, says Frank. His father recounted the tale of how his grandfather and Rupert became friends. Frank intended to inquire of Rupert on their next visit. He assured himself he would be their storyteller when they visited Elaine and Rupert.

5.2 A Planet Called Disco

After he got into the water, Derek's leg hurt. Aside from the capsule bobbing up and down like it was being lashed by waves, it appeared to him that he had crashed into an ocean filled with salty water and enormous white sharks.

Derek was on the planet DISC-0, nine light years away from Earth. Astronomers have discovered a planet named after a 20th-century rock star. His voice reverberated through the empty capsule, "Welcome to the Disco" with his groans echoing throughout the room. He let his seat belt off and took in the ocean's vastness. Several days ago, he was able to see nothing but the ocean as he soared above the Earth's surface. The area appears to be deserted. Not even on land or in the air. Not even a single bug or flying bird could be found here.

Something began to wiggle beneath Derek's feet as he finished his initial investigation. When Derek was ready, he stepped out of the capsule. He put on his helmet and gathered the items he'd need to build the platform for stability. Shocking noises may be heard coming from both sides of the spacecraft. Confused, he raised his head. Another hit was needed to rouse him from his slumber. The question is whether or not he was under attack. When his mind began to race, he scoured the cottage looking for a safe place to rest.

Thump. Again. Thump.

He made his way to the exit with a roll of duct tape in hand.

Unrolling some tape and holding it out to the unsuspecting guest, he stood there, scanning the landscape for the unwelcome visitor as if he were trying to patch up an air mattress's leaks. A flash of movement emerged from the water and made its way through the opening. "Hey!" In the capsule's center, Derek swiveled his head and saw a strange-looking monster. All of these terms are used interchangeably to describe a person who is fat. Round. Scales, fins, and a few protruding eyeballs make up this silver spherical. "Mearp" its mouth made a strange noise. While still holding his roll of tape, Derek shut the door and removed his helmet. In the meantime, the creature had settled in, mearing as it moved from area to area and scoured the bizarre circumstances it had found itself within. Derek lowered his defenses just as the disco ball swung at him with tremendous speed and agility. He immediately regretted the decision. Derek covered his eyebrows with his hands to protect what many people believed to be his best physical feature. As he raised his arms to fend off imaginary insects, he saw that the tape meant to keep him safe had been twisted in his hair and stuck to his face. At that moment, a strange thing pulled off Derek's face and hair and dropped it at his feet, glancing up at the spaceman. Before he screamed in anguish, Derek discovered that a large chunk of his hair and an eyebrow had been removed from his head and face. Despite this, Derek managed a half-smile as the disco ball revolved in the capsule. Derek gazed in awe at the possible wonders of his new home as a distant star appeared in the night sky, and the stabilizing platform sailed through the atmosphere. A friendly ball of scales found its way into his life, despite the loss of an eyebrow. Just in case, he kept a roll of duct tape handy.

An alarming rate of change was taking place in the situation. An enormous beast was rising from the depths, and Derek had no idea about it. Skyscraper-sized, with razor-sharp fangs protruding in all directions and a mouth large enough to swallow a double-decker bus, the creature emerged from the depths. As soon as the monster erupted from the surface, Derek's calm image turned into an uncontrollable storm of waves and roars. Suddenly, everyone and everything surged into the air as the stabilizing platform sprang into action. After seeing the beast below, Derek's stomach dropped as he realized that his impromptu trip and the knowledge that he was going to die were now one. This creature's teeth were clacking like the teeth of a thousand Japanese chefs sharpening a thousand Japanese knives. In an attempt to release himself from the beast's jaws, Derek fell to the ground, throwing his arms about like he was swimming. He dove into the water to get away with the teeth's stinging grip. In an effort to find Derek, the beast from the bottom screamed as it lowered itself to the depths. Unknown water depths claimed Derek's life. Disco ball was also looking for Derek at the same moment. As soon as it approached the astronaut's nearly lifeless body, it realized there was nothing it could do to revive him despite its best efforts. Astronauts can't be lifted and transported by this small animal. Suddenly, the disco ball had an idea and resurfaced. While still trying to get a glimpse of Derek, the giant beast in the sky grew more agitated. It was unable to get a good look at his body from below. Retreated into its murky depths after a final yell of victory in the name of evil and depravity. The disco ball rushed through the water in the meantime. By now, much of the bubble stream had gone, so it was more or less left to its own devices. While Derek lay still, the creature wrapped the duct tape around his arms and hands before entangling it in its own scales and dragging him to the surface. The Disco ball bounced on Derek's chest till it caused him to cough as they landed back on their feet. Derek's eyes opened wide, and he resumed breathing normally. Derek complimented his fish partner by untangling the duct tape from its scales once the foreign star had almost completely retreated. Derek let out a sigh of relief. When he set out to find a livable planet to take the place of the dying one so far away, things didn't go as planned. He may, however, have found a glimmer of hope for the planet's many inhabitants. His friend's silvery blue scales glowed with a shimmer that was as beautiful as the one emanating from his friend. It was a friendship that developed over time.

On the other hand, he wasn't the only one out there. It seemed to Derek that there was an unusual calmness in the air as he considered this. This pair of new pals — Derek and hope as a mirror ball – sat on Disco, a planet nine light years away from Earth, exchanging the final electromagnetic pulses.

5.3 Why the Autumn Leaves Are Red?

Once upon a time, only animals inhabited the planet, and they would occasionally hold great councils. The Bear, with his long claws, lustrous fur, and enormous roar, would be present, as would the Deer, who was so pleased with his antlers since they sprung from his head like trees, along with every other animal and bird. Also, Little Turtle will go there. She was so petite that she disliked conversing with others. She frequently wished, "Oh, if only I could perform a good deed! What could a small creature like me accomplish? Anyway" she thought "I'll be on the lookout, and perhaps one day I'll have an opportunity of doing something for my people". Little Turtle never forgot her intention to execute the nice deed. One day, the opportunity presented itself. "This place is pitch black; we can only see the Snowlight," the animals said as she sat in the Council chambers. It is also dismal. They said, "Couldn't we create a light and set it in Skyland?"

Little Turtle requested permission to ascend to Skyland. "I am confident that I can beam light up there". They indicated that she could perhaps go, and they contacted Dark Cloud to transport Little Turtle there. Dark Cloud arrived. Little Turtle observed that Lightning and Thunder were present in Dark Cloud. Upon arriving at Skyland, she fashioned the Sun from lightning and set it in the sky. The Sun was unable to move since it had no life, and the surface of the Earth was too hot to support life. "What shall we do?" the animals questioned. Someone stated, "We should give the Sun energy and vitality to go through the sky." Therefore, they granted him spirit and life, and he roamed the heavens. Mud Turtle created a hole in the ground for the Sun to pass through. Little Turtle created a wife for himself out of some of Dark Cloud's Lightning. She represented the Moon. Their young kids were the stars of Skyland's playgrounds. Little Turtle was taking good care of Skyland the entire time. The animals below referred to her as 'She Who Looks after Skyland.' She was quite thrilled since she was performing a nice action. Some animals felt envious of Little Turtle, especially the arrogant Deer with his antlers. One day, Deer requested Rainbow to transport him to Skyland, where Little Turtle resides. Rainbow wasn't sure if it was appropriate to take Deer to Little Turtle's home, but he said, "In the winter, while I rest on the large mountain near the lake, I will take you". It pleased the Deer. He did not inform anyone about Rainbow's pledge. He watched and waited near the large mountain for Rainbow to arrive all winter, but Rainbow never arrived. One day during the spring, Deer spotted a Rainbow by the lake. Why did you break your commitment to me, Rainbow? Rainbow made another promise to him. "When you see me in the dense fog, come to me beside the lake," he urged. The Deer also concealed this pledge since he wished to travel to Skyland alone. He waited at the lake every day. One day, when the dense fog rose from the lake, Deer spotted the magnificent Rainbow.

The rainbow formed an arch between the lake and the mountain. Then a bright light surrounded the deer, and he saw a clear route illuminated by the rainbow's colors. It traversed a vast forest. "Follow the way through the woodland," Rainbow instructed. The Deer followed the gleaming path, which brought him directly to Little Turtle's home in Skyland. And the Deer traversed all of Skyland. When the Great Council convened, Deer was absent. "The Deer has not arrived at the Council; where is the Deer?" A hawk soared all over the sky but could not locate Deer in the air. Wolf investigated the dense forests but was unable to locate any Deer. Rainbow had built a passage for Deer to climb to Skyland, which Little Turtle told the Council about when Dark Cloud brought him. "There it is," Little Turtle remarked. The animals surveyed the lake and spotted the picturesque trail there. They have never before seen it. "Why did Deer not wait for us?" "We should have all traveled to Skyland together", they added. Brown Bear was determined to take that path the next time he encountered it. While alone beside the lake one day, he spotted the gleaming trail that led across the vast forest. Soon after, he arrived at Skyland.

The first individual he encountered was a deer. "Why did you abandon us? Why did you go to Little Turtle's homeland without us? Why didn't you wait for us?" he inquired to the deer. The deer angrily shook his antlers. "What authority do you have to question me?" No one other than the Wolf may dispute my presence. "I shall execute you for your impudence." The deer stretched his neck, poised his antler-adorned head, and glowed with rage. The Bear lacked fear. His claws were keen and powerful, and his loud growls could be heard throughout Skyland. The conflict between the Deer and Bear shook Skyland. The creatures gazed upwards from the ground. "Who will go? Who will travel to Skyland to prohibit the Deer from fighting?" Wolf declared "I will leave. I am faster than anyone else." So, Wolf hurried along the gleaming route, and in a short time, he arrived at the battlefield. Wolf forced Deer to cease fighting. The antlers of the deer were coated in blood, and when he moved them, large drips fell through the air and splashed on the forest's leaves. The leaves turned a stunning shade of red. When the leaves turn crimson in the fall, the Deer and the Bear fought a tremendous war in Skyland, the land of Little Turtle, who was performing a good deed in the distant past.

5.4 The White Stone Canoe

Once upon a time, a very lovely Indian maiden died tragically on the day she was to marry a gorgeous young warrior. He was also courageous, but his heart was not immune to this loss. Since she was buried, he has felt neither joy nor tranquility. He frequently visited the location where the women had buried her and sat there contemplating, even though several of his comrades believed he would have been better off pursuing game or distracting himself on the battlefield. War and hunting were no longer appealing to him. His heart had already stopped beating. He disregarded his war club and bow and arrows and moved them out of the way.

He had heard that there was a way leading to the country of souls, and he was eager to follow it. Following this, he departed one morning after completing his travel arrangements. Initially, he was unsure of which direction to go. Only tradition dictated that he must travel south. For a time, he saw no change in the country's appearance. Forests, valleys, hills, and streams had the same appearance as in his homeland. There was lots of snow when he headed out, and occasionally it could be seen heaped and matted on the dense trees and bushes. Eventually, it began to fade and eventually vanished. Before he realized it, he found himself encircled by spring as the forest took on a brighter appearance and the leaves sprouted their buds. He had left the country of ice and snow behind. As the air grew milder and the winter clouds moved away, a clear blue sky appeared above him, and as he walked, he noticed flowers along the road and heard the melodies of birds. By these signals, he knew he was on the correct path, as they were consistent with his tribe's traditions. Eventually, he spotted a path. It brought him through a wood, up a long, raised slope, and to a lodge at the summit. At the door appeared an elderly guy with white hair and deep-set eyes that glowed with a burning brilliance. He held a stick and had a long robe of skins draped carelessly over his shoulders. The young Chippewayan started to narrate his narrative, but the elderly chief cut him off before he had spoken five words. "I had been expecting you," he said, "and had just rose to greet you at my residence. A few days ago, the individual you're looking for went through this area and rested due to travel tiredness. Enter my lodge and have a seat, and I will answer your questions and provide guidance for the remainder of your journey". Having accomplished this, they both proceeded to the lodge's entrance. "You see that gulf and the huge blue plains beyond," he remarked. It is the territory of souls. You are standing on its boundaries; my lodge is the access point. However, you cannot bring your body with you. "Leave it together with your arrows bundle, bow, and a dog. They will be secure upon your return". So stating, he re-entered the inn, and the released traveler leaped forward as if his feet were suddenly endowed with the ability to fly.

However, all items preserved their original hues and forms. The trees, plants, streams, and lakes were the most vibrant and beautiful he had ever seen. Animals leaped across his path with freedom and assurance, suggesting no blood had been shed here. Beautifully plumed birds inhabited the forests and frolicked in the rivers. There was only one instance in which he observed an extremely odd effect. He observed that his path was unimpeded by trees or other obstacles. He appeared to pass through them directly. In reality, they were the spirits or shadows of solid trees. He realized that he was in a world of darkness. When he had journeyed for a half-day through an ever-more-beautiful landscape, he reached the shores of a vast lake in the middle of a huge and lovely island. He discovered a white stone canoe tethered on the shore. He was confident that he had followed the correct way, as the elderly guy had informed him of this. In addition, there were gleaming paddles. He promptly entered the boat and took hold of the paddles when he saw the target of his search in another identical canoe, to his delight and amazement. She had mirrored his movements precisely, and they were next to each other. They immediately left the coast and began to traverse the lake. Its waves appeared to be rising, and from a distance, they appeared poised to engulf them; nevertheless, when they approached the whitened edge of the waves, animals seemed to vanish as if they were merely images of waves. However, no sooner had one wreath of foam passed than another, far more menacing one appeared. Thus, they lived in constant dread, which was compounded by the clarity of the water, from which they could observe heaps of dead creatures whose bones were scattered throughout the lakebed. However, the Master of Life had decided to let them through, as neither of their actions had been negative. Yet, they observed numerous more battling and drowning in the surf. There were old and young of various ages and ranks; some passed and others sank.   Only the young children's canoes appeared to encounter no waves. Eventually, every obstacle vanished instantly, and they both leaped onto the blissful island. They believed that the air itself was food. It nourished and strengthened them. Together, they traversed the idyllic fields, where everything was designed to satisfy the eye and ear. There were no storms, ice, or cold winds; no one trembled for lack of warm clothing; no one was hungry, and no one lamented the deceased. They did not observe any graves. They knew nothing of wars. There's no hunting because their nourishment was the air itself. The young warrior would have stayed there forever if he could, but he had to return to retrieve his body. He could not see the Lord of Life but heard his voice in a gentle breeze. This voice said, "Return to the country from which you came. Your moment has not yet arrived. The obligations I assigned to you and must do are not yet complete. Return to your tribe and fulfill your responsibilities as a good man. You will dominate your tribe for an extended period. My messenger, who guards the entrance, will communicate the regulations you must follow. He will instruct you on what to do when he returns your body. After listening to him, you will rejoin the spirit that you must now abandon behind. She is welcomed and will remain here forever, as young and content as when I first summoned her from the country of snows." The narrator awoke after this voice ceased. It was all a dream, and he remained in a world of cold snows, hunger, and sorrow.

5.5 The Great White Bear and the Trolls

Once upon a time, a man named Halvor in Finmark owned a large white bear skilled in many stunts. The guy thought to himself one day, "What a gorgeous bear. The King of Denmark will receive it as a present from me, and he may also decide to give me an entire bag of cash in return".

122

Therefore, he went off for Denmark while dragging the bear after him. He traveled on and on, and after some time, he arrived at a dense, dark forest. As it was almost dusk and no home was in sight, Halvor began to fear that he might be forced to sleep on the ground beneath the trees.

Nevertheless, he heard the noise of a woodcutter's ax at that moment. Following the sound, he arrived at a clearing in the trees. Indeed, there was a man diligently chopping down trees. "And wherever there is a man, there must be a home for him," Halvor reasoned. "Good day," remarked Halvor. The man responded, "Good day!" while peering intently at the enormous white bear. "Will you give my bear and I refuge for the night?" Halvor inquired. "Will you also provide us with some food? I will compensate you generously if you will." The guy said, "I would be more than happy to provide you with both food and shelter; however, tonight, of all nights in the year, no one may stop at my home unless they are willing to take the danger of their lives". Halvor was astonished and questioned, "How is that even possible?", "Why is it this way? It is the eve of St. John, and every troll in the forest comes to my house on St. John's Eve. They eat and drink all night, so I have to make dinner for them. They would definitely tear him apart if they found anyone inside the house right now. My wife and I cannot stay, even. "We must spend a night in the woods." Halvor declared, "This is an odd business". "However, I'm considering stopping there to see what these trolls look like. Regarding the prospect of them inflicting damage on me,

I have no fear once I have my bear with me. The woodcutter was taken aback upon hearing this and said, "No, don't do that! Spend the night with us out here in the woods and we can go back safe and sound tomorrow".

However, Halvor would not listen. In addition to his determination to rest in a house that night, he was curious to see what trolls seemed like. Since you are willing to sacrifice your life, the woodcutter advised, "Follow that road, and it will lead you directly to my residence." Halvor thanked him and left, and soon he and his bear reached the woodcutter's home. He opened the door and stepped inside, and when he saw the meal the woodcutter had made for the trolls, he felt very hungry. There were sausages, ale, salmon, cakes, rice porridge, and all sorts of delightful dishes. He tried some out and gave some to his bear, and then sat on the ground to wait for the trolls to come. As for the bear, he laid down beside his master and drifted off to sleep.

They hadn't been there long when a roar emanated from the trees. It sounded like moaning, groaning, whistling, and screeching. It grew so loud and terrifying that Halvor was overcome with fear. The chill crawled up and down his back, causing his hair to rise. The sound grew closer and closer until it reached the door, at which point Halvor could no longer withstand it. He sprung up from his seat and quickly made his way to the oven. He swung open the door and stepped inside, shutting the door behind him.

However, the big white bear paid little attention and only snored in his sleep. Halvor had hardly stepped into the oven when the front door of the house burst open and all the forest trolls poured into the room. There were both big and small trolls, both fat and skinny.There were some with extremely long tails, some with shorter tails, and some without any tail. Some had two eyes, some had three, and some had a single eye in the middle of their forehead. One person, called Long Nose, had a nose that was as long and thin as a poker. The trolls pounded on the door as they entered and swarmed around the feasting table. The biggest troll roared in a frightening voice, "What is this?" Halvor's heart quaked. "Someone was here before us. The food has been tasted and the beer has been spilled." Immediately, Long Nose started to sniff around, looking for clues "Whoever was here before is still here" he shouted. Let's find him and tear him apart. "By the way, this is his little cat," the littlest troll said, pointing to the white bear. "Oh, what a lovely kitty!"

Then, the small troll put a piece of sausage on a fork and pressed it against the white bear's snout. The large white bear let out a roar and rose up. The bear swatted the troll with his paw, sending him flying across the room. His long nose was almost cut off, and the big troll's ears echoed with the package he got. The bear pounded and flailed the trolls in all directions until they ripped open the door and ran away into the woods while screaming with terror. Once all the others had gone, Halvor scurried out of the cave, closing the door behind him. He and the white bear then sat down and ate to their hearts' delight.

They settled down and had a peaceful sleep for the rest of the night. The woodcutter and his family crept back to the house and peered in the window in the early morning. It was a shock to see Halvor and his bear sitting there and happily having their breakfasts as if nothing had happened.

The woodcutter exclaimed, "What gives? Did the trolls not come?" Halvor replied, "Yes, they did, but we took them away and I don't think they'll bother you again." He then told the woodcutter what had happened during the night.

He said, "After the hard time they went through, they will be reluctant to come back" causing the woodcutter to feel overwhelmed with joy and gratitude.

He and his wife begged Halvor to stay in the woods and stay with them, but Halvor refused. He was on his way to Denmark to trade his bear to the King and he was determined to carry on to Denmark. After they said their farewells, he left, taking with him the fond wishes of the woodcutter and his wife.

The following year, on St. John's Eve, the woodcutter was cutting down trees in the forest when a huge, ugly troll came out of a nearby tree. "Woodcutter! Carpenter!" he bellowed. The woodcutter questioned, "What do you want?" "Say, do you still possess that big white cat?" "Indeed I do; in addition, she now has five kittens, each one larger and stronger than her." "Is that true?" yelled the dreadful troll.

Then, goodbye woodcutter, as we will never come back to your house. After that, he tucked in his head, the tree shut and the woodcutter never heard or spotted the trolls again. After that, he and his family were living in harmony and without worry.

Halvor had already arrived in Denmark, and the King was very pleased with the bear he had brought. So much so that he gave Halvor a sack full of money as a reward. Halvor used this money to invest in trading and was soon one of the wealthiest men in Denmark.

Conclusion

Your top priority as a parent is your child's health and well-being. When you give nutritious meals, you take care of your child's health, and a secure and healthy atmosphere will ensure their well-being. In addition to this, parents want their children to develop into decent adults.

Numerous parents often read or share bedtime stories with their kids. Typically, they see it as an enjoyable hobby. The only thing most parents need to remember is that sharing or telling bedtime stories can also play a significant role in personality development.

Young children are comparable to clay. We can shape their personalities and cognitive processes as we see fit; bedtime stories are an effective method. Children see their parents as mentors and attempt to imitate their behavior.

Similarly, kids are motivated by their parents' ideas and try to emulate them. If they listen to and converse with their elders about morality, values, life skills, and problem-solving skills, these key skills and values will penetrate their systems and make them better people.

Is it not an amazing thing? Make bedtime reading sessions a daily occurrence for individuals who have not yet. Plant the seeds, and you will reap various advantages

Printed in Great Britain
by Amazon

22730110R00076